CHRISTMAS KRINGLE: SILENT NIGHT

LMBPN Publishing
PMB 196, 2540 South Maryland Pkwy
Las Vegas, NV 89109

First US Edition, December 2020
Version 1.01, December 2020

eBook ISBN: 978-1-64971-361-2
Print ISBN: 978-1-64971-351-3

CHRISTMAS KRINGLE: SILENT NIGHT

CHRISTMAS KRINGLE™ BOOK ONE

MICHAEL ANDERLE

THE CHRISTMAS KRINGLE: SILENT
KNIGHT TEAM

Thanks to the JIT Readers

Debi Sateren
Dave Hicks
Peter Manis
Micky Cocker
Dorothy Lloyd
Daryl McDaniel
Deb Mader
Misty Roa
Rachel Beckford
Jeff Goode
Diane L. Smith
Wendy L Bonell
Jackey Hankard-Brodie
Angel LaVey
Veronica Stephan-Miller
Paul Westman

If I've missed anyone, please let me know!

Editor
The Skyhunter Editing Team

DEDICATION

To Family, Friends and
Those Who Love
To Read.
May We All Enjoy Grace
To Live The Life We Are
Called.

—Michael

CHAPTER ONE

Some people complained about driving in winter. They were understandably concerned about snow making the roads more dangerous.

Still, it was Nova Scotia. People here were used to snow appearing near the end of the year, and he was more accustomed to it than most.

Sure, he was facing a few challenges besides the weather. He needed a firm cushion that would let him reliably see over the wheel, plus pedal extenders to accommodate his shorter legs. It was the modern day now, and there were more than a few gadgets available that allowed little people to drive.

He liked driving in the snow. It felt almost natural, which was odd. He was comfortable driving when there was no snow as well, although rain and sleet could be a problem.

Snow was comfortable. He could keep going through it all day, and it felt like he had. With only a week until Christmas, people wanted too much from a comptroller on the Halifax Regional Council. The worst of it, interestingly, was that people wanted him to plan the Christmas parties that would happen all over the building he worked in.

Veris had no idea why people assumed he liked planning Christmas parties. He did, but planning twelve of them, one for each separate division, had been just plain exhausting.

Today had been the last one, as well as the last day of work before the Christmas break, during which he would need to plan another Christmas party. He didn't mind that one as much. His family would be a lot more helpful than the party planning committee at work, and Helen would be making most of the calls anyway.

There were still celebrations in order, though, and Veris found himself smiling as he pulled his car to a halt in the parking lot illuminated by a large neon sign, showing two men clinking glasses and downing them with alternating lighting.

Below the two men, the sign told him that he had just arrived at Noel's Tavern. Not the most creative of names, but they weren't looking for any kind of viral marketing at this point. It was one of the oldest bars in the area, which meant they had more than their fair share of regulars and underground notoriety.

Noel, the owner, would not be hurting for clientele for a while. Veris was one of the regulars who was making sure of that.

He pushed his way through the doors, taking a deep breath before pulling his coat off.

It was a little early, so most of the booths were still

empty, with only a handful of patrons sitting at the bar and following a local hockey game.

"I'm going to take one of the booths, Mikey," Veris said, waving to get the bartender's attention.

"No problem, Ver. I'll be with you shortly," the man replied, eliciting a round of snickers from the men at the bar.

"Blow-ho-ho me," Veris replied, offering Mikey his middle finger in response.

That got a laugh from the barkeep, who shook his head as he filled a tall mug at the tap for a frothy lager. "You couldn't afford me, Veris. There's someone waiting for you. Asked for you by name, too. Not a lot of people that can pronounce Veris Charo... Cha..."

"Czarodziejski," Veris corrected the man, taking his mug after it was placed on the counter. "It's Polish. Try being a little tuned in to other cultures."

"I'm all for foreign cultures until they try to get a full fucking alphabet into my mouth. Anyways, he's waiting for you in the corner booth."

Veris turned as he took a sip from his beer and immediately regretted it. The sight of the man waiting for him made him cough most of the cool liquid back up.

"You okay?"

Veris waved the bartender away, shaking his head as he walked over to the corner booth. Of all the people he'd expected to see before Christmas day, Kris was not among them.

He didn't look the part. Even with the thick gray sweater the man was wearing, the edges of the tattoos that covered his body were clearly visible, ending a few inches beyond the cuff on the back of the man's hand. There was no bowl full of jelly around his midsection, which was tight and well-exercised, and the pristine white beard didn't take away from the overall menace of the man sitting at the table.

The short hair, also a pristine white, was enough to take away any softness the beard might have added to his features—that or the icy blue eyes.

"Nick," Veris said, not sure if he was supposed to say the man's name aloud. "Of all the gin joints in all the towns and all that. How the hell are you?"

"Been better," Kris said, shaking his head, then downing what was left of his drink. "And you can just call me Kris. Should, even."

"But it's your title."

"And I am away from the North Pole. Out here, I'm just Kris."

Mikey was there with a refill in place of the empty drink, leaving a glass of cranberry juice in front of Kris.

"What, did they not have a glass of milk for you?"

Mikey narrowed his eyes, confused but not making any comment as he retreated back behind the bar where the rest of the regulars were shouting about something happening in the game.

"I didn't think to find you around here this time of year," Veris continued, taking another sip of his beer. "Or has the mechanization of the workforce in the workshop been so effective that you don't need to be around come the holidays?"

"That is the idea, but we are not quite there yet," Kris replied. "We still need to have a few elves in place to maintain the machinery I brought in. Only the ones who wanted to stay, of course. The rest of you went off to live your own lives. How are things here?"

"I'll never complain about having a life. As much as I might miss working in the workshop with you and the rest, I...well, I've found my own family to bring presents to."

"Really?"

Kris leaned forward as Veris produced his phone and showed him pictures of Helen, Holly, and Brian, the latter two sporting the elf costumes he'd gotten for them.

"I'm happy for you," Kris replied, smiling as he handed the elf his phone back. "Most of the others were able to hit the ground running as well."

"I was surprised you had contacts with the Canadian government, and they were able to find work for us all. How the hell does a former mercenary have connections? In Canada, of all places?"

"It...is not a pretty story, and not part of my life anymore. I am glad it turned out to have something of a happy ending. You lot deserve it."

"Might I ask you what I'm sure is an odd question?"

Kris nodded, running his fingers through his beard.

"Brian and Holly. I mean, I know you can't say until the day comes, but which list did they end up on this year? Can you give me a hint? I mean, Holly is mine, and I adopted Brian, and I am trying to be a good father to both of them. Hard to say how well I've done so far."

The white-haired man smirked. "Well, I can tell you they won't be getting coal this year, but I won't say anything else. There need to be a *few* surprises come Christmas morning."

"Of course, of course."

"You are doing a fantastic job with them, Veris. Which is, I suppose, why you wouldn't be able to help me with the trouble I find myself in."

"Oh, right." Veris took a sip from his beer. "I forgot. What brings you around here less than a week from the big day?"

Kris scowled down at his glass, toying with the straw. Veris had never seen the man this way. He barely looked contained, and the worst part was that he was sitting, sipping, and talking like there was nothing wrong, while his eyes were a very particular kind of dead. Only someone who had known him before would be aware that he was anything other than one of those weirdos who had cranberry juice at a bar while the rest of the place was getting their buzz on.

Or maybe he was a designated driver of some sort. Veris would be taking a cab home and come out for a brisk walk to pick his vehicle up tomorrow. Helen didn't mind as long as he was the one who made breakfast early the next morning.

"Well, I'll come right out and say it," Kris muttered. "The sleigh—it's been stolen."

Veris almost coughed up another gulp of beer. "*What?*"

"You heard me. Someone stole the damn thing. Well, I have a few leads as to who might have pulled that sort of bullshit, but they've gone underground. I can go after them, but my experience tells me that when someone lays out crumbs for me to follow, it's because they want me to. It's probably a trap."

"It's easy to forget that you of all people have experience

with this sort of thing," Veris noted. "I agree about the trap thing. But wait, if they took the sleigh, how the hell did you get here?"

"They took the new one, with all the presents already loaded and ready to go."

"You have the presents loaded and ready to go a week before the big day?" The elf raised an eyebrow. "Maybe mechanizing the whole process *was* a good idea."

"It was. But no amount of mechanizing will allow me to get replacement presents ready in six days, and I need to find the thieves, so...well, I took the old sleigh."

Veris smirked, shaking his head. "I bet Rudy and the gang weren't happy about that. Pretty sure they've been enjoying retirement almost as much as we have."

"You would be correct about that assumption, but he understands the problems we're facing here. He also understands that our travel range is limited, considering all the radar stations that would be able to detect us if we set so much as a hoof in American airspace. Almost shot us out of the sky the last time around. Folks have been a lot more trigger-happy since 9/11, and I can't say I blame them."

"I thought you had an agreement with the government?"

"The Canadian government," Kris noted. "They don't mind me making my rounds in their airspace, but the rest of the world has a problem with an unknown flying object. That was why we either needed to upgrade or get an agreement from all the governments in the world to allow us to come around once a year. I figured that going the technological route was more realistic."

The elf laughed. "Having worked in local government

for the past five years, I'd say you're correct in that assumption. I still have no idea how you managed to get the Canadian government to agree with you on it."

"I've got connections. My predecessor likely wouldn't have been able to get the agreement, but...well, the folks manning the radar stations don't mind a friendly flying around. Not that they would have picked it up with the new sleigh, which is why I need to recover it."

"I really do wish I could help," Veris said.

"That would be nice, but you have your family to care for. Besides, this was more about checking in and speaking to the rest of you beforehand."

"You think you won't make it back?" Veris whispered.

"I've been on enough...recovery missions to know there is a possibility that someone new will have to be selected for the job before the week is out, but that's not the point. My point is...well, remembering in part why I chose this line of work. I might have to dive back into what I genuinely enjoyed about my past life, and a reminder of the reasons why I left it are...well, they are appreciated."

Veris found himself smiling as he looked down at his mug. It wasn't that he'd disliked the man who'd formerly carried the title, although he remembered little about him. He had been good enough, but unremarkable, which many thought was a good trait for the man who wore the red suit. The changes and vision Kris had brought to the position were refreshing. He'd saved the holiday in many ways, and the holiday had saved him as well.

Christmas would be the poorer for losing him.

"Well, I hope you find the bastards," Veris finally said, watching Kris' slow, deliberate movements in raising his glass to his lips and taking a sip. "I'm not sure what they hope to gain by trying to get you out in the open like that."

"Could be a terrorist group," Kris answered, inspecting his drink. "Looking to kill me or parade me around as a statement of their authority."

"I thought you said you knew who did this?"

"I said I had leads, and I have a few ideas, but dropping into an investigation like this with preconceptions is dangerous, and it could waste a lot of valuable time. They left me a trail, and I'll follow it with an open mind."

"I thought you said that it was probably a trap?"

"It probably is."

"And yet, your idea is to—"

"Spring the trap, yes."

Veris shook his head. "Did you do that often in your past life?"

"More than you'd think. In the end, letting people think you're trapped is the most reliable way to get them to lower their guard."

"With the downside of you ending up...trapped."

"Sure, but not as trapped as they might think. I've come away with the advantage every time it's happened in the past."

"Just takes the one time you're wrong, though."

Kris scowled and nodded.

"You want a drink?" Veris asked. "I can pick up a round for you. A way to celebrate and steel yourself for what you have to do."

"Rudy wouldn't stand for it." Kris took another sip of his cranberry juice. "He's insisting that I stay on the wagon, literally and metaphorically, if we're going to do this together."

"Well, if that's the case, I'll toast you on your way with cranberry juice." Veris winced as the words left his mouth but raised his glass anyway. "It'll be tough, but I hope you drop the bastards, Kris. I mean, stealing St. Nicholas' sleigh six days before Christmas is just asking for it."

"Hear, hear," Kris chimed in, tapping his glass to Veris'.

CHAPTER TWO

He'd forgotten how cold it got on the old sleigh. Certain measures could be taken if he needed them, of course, but he was still sitting in a sleigh with no roof, making his way through what was easily one of the coldest areas in the world.

Rudy brought the reindeer team into a descent, heading straight into the wind that was driving into them. The sleigh's design allowed it to cut through the air easily, and Kris hunched inside, trying to keep himself out of the wind, letting Rudy and the others guide it in.

Truth be told, they were probably better at flying the damn thing than he was. Having his hands on the reins was a formality. He could feel that the team was pulling well despite the cold and wind as they headed to the landing strip outside the workshop. It was as light a landing as it could be, though Kris did feel a jolt through his body as they touched down.

"Son of a bitch!" he hissed, keeping himself steady in his

seat as they slowed down over the snow. Once they were at an acceptable speed, Kris jumped lightly out of the sleigh and moved down the line, quickly releasing the reindeer from their harness.

When he arrived at the front of the line, Kris patted Rudy on the neck before releasing his straps. The reindeer's nose was still steaming from the snow melting on it.

Rudy snorted and nudged him.

"I know that wasn't your fault," Kris muttered, shaking his head. "I wasn't braced for the landing like I should have been. Been a few years since we got the new sleigh, and I wasn't ready for the old one anymore."

The reindeer grumbled as they headed toward the barn where the team was spending the winter, although Kris had been looking for a place for them to spend their retirement that wasn't in the North Pole. It seemed like the right thing to do.

"No, I don't think you're rusty at leading the team," Kris answered. "The whole team is as good as you were the last Christmas we headed out. It's all me, I guarantee it."

The reindeer wasn't convinced, but he was tired and didn't feel like arguing about it anymore. He stepped into the barn with the rest.

"I'll check on you guys later," Kris promised as he closed the doors. It wasn't like they couldn't leave if they wanted to, but with the icy winter they were experiencing, there was little call to leave the comfort and warmth of their barn.

Kris could relate. He pulled his collar up against the wind as he headed toward the workshop.

As buildings went, it wasn't that impressive. It was even smaller than the barn and looked like a small house, barely large enough to accommodate a small family. The exterior was weather-beaten but sturdy, designed to withstand the heavy winds that whipped across the open area around the North Pole.

The interior was even sturdier, reinforced with enough armor to withstand a direct nuclear blast. The storms they faced in the winter were paltry by comparison.

The door opened as he approached and closed quickly behind him to keep the cold out. The reinforced secondary door remained locked as it quickly scanned him to confirm his identity.

It didn't take long, but the security protocol did need to be followed, now more than ever.

After the verification was performed, the safety door opened to allow him access to the interior.

Most of the workspace was in an underground bunker, hidden from most, if not all, who sought its location, either for their own purposes or to sell the information to the highest bidder.

The elevator took him down for a solid minute, heading deep into the ground until he felt the heat coming from the generators below. They got a little of their power from fans above the ground, but there were generators underground he'd never had access to that provided most of the power for the building. The Workshop had a way of putting things together when he wasn't paying attention.

He had asked questions when he first took up the red coat, but none had been answered. He had come to accept that there were many things in this place that did not fall within his narrow view of the world. It had been difficult to find his way here, but after everything that had happened, desperation had paved roads he'd never thought he would have to travel.

The Workshop had a mind of its own. There was no point in investigating further—not that he didn't try from time to time, but he never assumed his searches would produce results.

Most of the machines in the workshop were powered down for the season, although a few of the elves still remained to perform spot checks on them to make sure that there were no surprises when the next season rolled around.

One of them looked up from his work and pulled off a pair of soldering goggles when he saw Kris approaching.

"We got that kink fixed in the assembly line's conveyor," he said, picking up a bottle of water. "Grease was gunking up the works and loosening the screws inside. If we hadn't caught it early, the whole thing would have worn down, and we'd have had to get new parts delivered. Thankfully, we were able to make do with the parts that we have."

"Nice work," Kris said, looking around. A dozen or so other elves were still working.

"Yes, well, you don't keep us around for our singing voices."

"I mean, your singing voices *are* worth it. Your mechanical skills are good too, considering you've kept this place in business for the past three centuries."

"Four if you count Grenie," the elf noted, pointing at one of the elves.

Kris eyed her. It was difficult to determine which was which when they were in their uniforms. Grenie was one of the oldest elves around, but there was no sign of aging in any of them.

"Hope I look that good at four hundred years old," Kris muttered, running his fingers through his beard. "How long have you been here, Valy?"

"My first Christmas working on the line was 1876." Valy pulled his hat off and wiped the sweat from his forehead. "Compared to some of the others, I'm quite young and fresh at this work. The ones that retired, they were never much good at keeping the machines running. Best that they headed off and lived their lives far away from where we're keeping the holiday in place."

"I wouldn't say they were terrible."

"I would."

Kris smirked and nodded. "Fair enough, but that's only because I'm relying on you youngsters to keep everything running the way it was meant to."

"The way it was meant to was us working our hands to the bone, providing presents for over two-point-two billion children." Valy replaced his cap and shuddered. "I don't think we would ever have been able to keep up with that. Mechanizing the process made it all a lot simpler, easier, and more efficient. Hell, I don't think we were ever able to finish the work this early, even when there were only a quarter of a billion children around the world. You really are quite ingenious."

"You know it wasn't actually me, right?" Kris asked as they headed over to the other side of the manufacturing floor, where his office was situated. "All that happened because the Workshop decided you folks needed some help."

"No help was offered under the old Santa, bless his soul," Valy replied with a shrug. "The Workshop gets its inspiration from your mind, and you gave it the idea of modernizing the place."

They kept saying that, but Kris never understood what they were talking about. It was a little odd to be told he was somehow connected to the Workshop, and it was taking all the information he had to offer while giving nothing back.

There was no point in thinking about it. He didn't have control of what was happening either way, and he had given up thinking there was any point in digging into what was going on around him.

Besides, the elves appeared to be a great deal more connected to the workshop than he was, or at least to the magic that drove it.

"What have you been up to?" Valy asked as they approached the office. "Noticed you took the old sleigh out for a spin. Were the reindeer really that desperate for some exercise?"

"I wouldn't say desperate, but it *had* been a long time since they took the lead out there," Kris pointed out, pulling the door open and holding it open for his foreman to enter the office before he did. "There were a few things I needed to do out in the world before the holiday, and it seemed like it would be a mistake to take the new sleigh, considering we've already loaded it with all the presents."

"Fair enough. Besides, if something were to go wrong

with the new one, it's always good to have the old one on hand, wouldn't you say, boss?"

Having them call him that was a little irksome. He didn't give them orders or even tell them what to do. His job revolved around keeping track of the lists and delivering the presents. The whole process between the lists and the delivery was on them, and he had clued in early that they didn't need much direction on what they needed to do.

If anything, him micro-managing would slow their process down, and there was no point in that unless he had something to add.

He *had* corrected them about calling him boss, or even St. Nick, but they didn't take his word for that either. They just kept working. As far as he could tell, they saw him as a figurehead.

It was a little odd that they kept thinking of him as their boss, though.

"Is everything all right, boss?"

Kris flinched visibly at the word. "No, not really."

The office was a nice place, with panels in the back showing a variety of different screens, with a mahogany desk in the center, a half-dozen elf-sized chairs on one side, and a Kris-sized office chair on the other. A couch filled the far wall. That was made for folk with longer legs, although the elves had no trouble using it when there were no more seats available in their size.

Valy moved to one of the chairs made for elves and hopped into it as Kris took his seat behind the desk.

The screens showed a variety of different locations

from the snowy conditions outside to forests, jungles, and beaches.

He used the screens to keep track of the lists, but at this point, the lists for the year were complete, and all he could do was wait for next year's lists to start showing up.

For now, though, it looked like Valy was waiting for him to tell him what was wrong. The elf was sitting calmly, not pressuring Kris, but definitely not moving from his seat.

"Nothing really," Kris stated, shaking his head. "Just went out to meet a few of the others who are getting on with their lives. Wondering what that was like."

"You could always just do so."

Kris shook his head. "Not yet, and not for a good long while, either. No need to worry about me. I'll be back in the spirit of things before you know it."

"Well, then." Valy jumped lightly from his seat. "I'll just make sure the rest of the machinery is in top shape. I'll get the reports in to you tomorrow morning if that works."

Kris nodded.

"Merry Christmas, Kris, and check out the presents the Workshop left for you," the elf said, doffing his hat, winking, and moving toward the door. "Open or closed?"

"Closed, please." Kris was already out of his seat. There were a handful of gifts wrapped and waiting for him on the sofa.

He moved over to them. Sure, presents from the damn Workshop. Maybe it knew what happened to the sleigh and was giving him clues? It was odd for it to be doling presents out this early.

Although the elves never questioned it—another odd

thing about them. He would like to talk to Veris about it sometime, but it always felt like it was not an appropriate topic. The elf was making a life for himself, which meant that a conversation about his work at the Workshop for the previous three decades felt like it needed to be held in the right setting, away from prying eyes.

He pulled the wrapping off the presents, narrowing his eyes as a metal briefcase was revealed, and a second holding a suit of top-of-the-line body armor, the kind he had never been able to afford back in the day.

"Well, I guess that means you know what I need to get into the fight, eh?" Kris asked aloud, looking around the room. He didn't expect an answer, but he tried it occasionally just to make sure.

The operational necessities were all in the briefcase: a low-caliber scoped rifle with a suppressor, a pistol with the same, a combat knife, and a handful of the other accouterments he generally procured new before each mission, which could be discarded if he needed to.

Maybe the Workshop *could* hear him, although its failure to talk back was more than a little annoying.

Kris settled down in front of his desk and pulled an old razor out of one of the drawers. He needed to tend to a few different rituals before he headed out into the field again, and the first one was shaving his head clean. Old habits died hard.

Not for any real purpose, of course, but simply because it was what he was used to. The beard remained, however.

"Boss?"

Kris was almost finished. He was working on the back

of his neck, using one of the screens as a mirror to assist him.

"How can I help you, Valy?" Kris asked, carefully gliding the razor over his skin.

"Is...is everything all right?"

Kris took a deep breath as he looked at the familiar yet foreign features staring at him from the screen.

"Not by a long shot," he said softly. "But it will be soon."

CHAPTER THREE

There was no telling why people liked to be in the swelteringly hot places in the world.

Or at least, Kris would never understand it. The places were cursed to be covered in insects, reptiles, and the kind of humidity that made sure that one would never be able to dry off correctly, but in the end, people still flocked to the locations to enjoy the sun and the salt water of the ocean.

There were other reasons to spend time in the Bahamas, of course. Kris could think of more than a dozen as he sipped a cool glass of coconut water. He was looking out the window, eyeing the beach, which was filling up with the local population, as well as tourists.

If one had an interest in marine wildlife, it was a fantastic place to be in. There was also the interesting culture of the area, as well as the favorable tax laws, and the presence of at least a dozen all-inclusive, adults-only resorts that drew in the tourists all year round.

Kris found himself more interested in the laws that made the place a tax haven, of course.

"Kris, is there anything you'd like to eat?" a woman's voice asked from deep inside the house. "I think I can whip a little something up before the maid comes along. She's got a lot to do today, so I don't want to overwhelm her with chores."

"I'm fine, Mother," Kris growled, then took another sip of the cool, refreshing coconut water. His parents hadn't been in a position to retire in their old age, meaning that it had fallen to him to make sure that they didn't have to keep working. He wasn't going to use the profits from his previous life, and while most of it went to charity, a good portion found its way into a variety of funds that had allowed the two to settle down in comfort and relative luxury during their twilight years.

They had nothing to do with what he'd been in the past. If anything, they were the ones who had driven him to do something else with his life. They deserved the break.

"Well, I'll make you something anyway," his mother shouted back. "It's been a while since I've made my world-famous chili. You love it!"

It was weird how everyone in the world had a world-famous chili recipe.

"Fine, Mother!" he shouted back, looking at the phone the Workshop had provided him.

The operation was funded out of the Bahamas—Nassau, to be specific. That couldn't be a coincidence, which made things that much more dangerous. It was one thing for people to be gunning for Santa Claus, quite another for them to be after Kristian Kringle.

It meant that they knew *who* he was, not just what.

"Did you like it with overcooked or undercooked

onions, honey?" his mother called.

"Undercooked onions," Kris shouted back. "Do you need me to come in there and help you?"

"Screw that. I know you're busy. I just want to make sure you're eating right. It's not natural for your hair and beard to suddenly go white like that. Have you seen a doctor about it?"

"Yeah, it was...stress."

Not his best lie, but then he'd never felt comfortable lying to the woman.

He'd had to take a commercial flight to Nassau, which had put him at risk. Then again, bringing the sleigh down was not an option, not after that little encounter he'd had with the US military drones about a decade prior.

They hadn't been able to shoot him down, but the fact that he had even registered on their scanners was concerning. He was lucky they hadn't knocked him down with surface-to-air missiles.

Of course, they'd covered the whole thing up and eventually released the pictures as a UFO stunt, but the incident still stung.

"I'm just so happy to have you around again." The woman left the kitchen, came over to where he was sitting, and wrapped him up in a hug without so much as letting him stand up to return it. He resorted to patting her arms gently.

"I'm glad to see you guys, too," he mumbled.

"I know, and it's your new job that's telling on you. You were on edge before, but the stress turning all your hair white? Now, that's just ridiculous."

She headed back to the kitchen, putting her graying

hair in a loose braid as a man entered the room.

His head was bald as well, although it was less of a choice for him. There was no beard, though. He'd worked as an accountant all his life, and had thought the whole gym fad was malarkey—his own words—and had gone into his sixties looking leaner than his son, although he had put on a few pounds since Kris had last seen him.

"Still haven't told her what you're doing, then?" his father asked, taking a seat across the table from Kris.

"If you figure out a way to describe it that doesn't get me locked up in the nearest padded cell, you let me know."

Kringle Senior smirked and shook his head. "I'm not sure *I* believe it. It does seem to do you good, though. Hair notwithstanding, you look more...at peace. Although you lifting those ridiculous weights just boggles my mind."

"I guess I should just let myself go and sport a bowl full of jelly around my midsection like the whole world thinks I do?"

"Not to that point, of course, but you don't need to have the workout regimen of an Olympic gymnast to be healthy."

"It's a military regimen, and it looks like you've been eating plenty healthy for both of us."

"Asshole," his father grumbled with a hint of humor in his eyes. "It's the maid your mom picked out. She insists on cooking our meals—she's one damn fine cook too—but she deep-fries just about everything she gets her hands on."

"I've never heard of a man from Georgia complaining about too much deep-fried food."

"Hey, I've been to my share of cookouts and cooked pretty much anything by dipping it into a vat full of cooking oil. You both love my fried chicken, right? Still, everything in moderation. It's like the woman's trying to give me a heart attack or something."

"Have you talked to her about it?"

"Sure, but old habits die hard, I guess. The food is pretty damn tasty, too. You should try her fried bananas."

"I don't think I'll be in Nassau long enough."

His father nodded, then tilted his head to the side and reached up to play with the hair that was no longer there before snapping his hand back down. Old habits.

"You're working again, then?"

Kris watched the older man from the corner of his eye. They'd both managed to keep what Kris had done for a living in the past a secret, although it had been difficult for both of them. A fair share of arguments and yelling matches had resulted, but if there was one thing he could be with his father, it was utterly honest.

The only reason he had to lie was to keep his mother's expectations for him from being dashed to pieces. There was no such restriction with his father, mostly because it had been his accounting connections that had gotten Kris into the merc business, although neither man anticipated the dark path that career choice would end up leading him down.

"I'm just happy he's not traveling all over the world like he used to," his mother said, coming back out of the kitchen smelling like chopped onions. "Flying all over the place for business trips just has to be bad for you. Moving from time zone to time zone. Heaven forbid you ever need to get into that sort of business again."

His father raised an eyebrow as she retreated out of

earshot.

"Are you? Working again, I mean?"

"Just the one job. Got people counting on me for it, and it shouldn't last very long."

"I've heard that line before." His father shook his head and reached for a pack of the cigarettes he'd quit smoking three years ago. "Hope you stick to it this time."

"Me too. Has anyone been around here asking for me? Me specifically, by name."

His father shook his head. "I can't say anyone has. We don't get a lot of visitors out here, so I think I'd remember if someone came around."

Kris scowled. It was too much to hope that the thieves had exposed themselves. Even a middleman would allow him to track down the people who had hired him.

Still, it was worth a shot.

"Tell Mom I'll be back later for the chili. I need to get a coffee."

He had scouted this place for a few days before deciding his parents could move into the city. It was always a good idea to make sure that there wasn't some sort of catastrophe headed their way, but aside from hurricane season, which he'd accounted for by making sure they were in a solidly-built house with a generator and protective systems in place, the island was paradise.

Of course, there were all sorts of random occurrences that could hit them, but that was true of almost anywhere in the world at this point.

During that time of inspection, he'd frequented one of the local coffee shops, which made some of the best coffee that he had ever tasted. He wasn't sure how they managed that since he had traveled all over the world and tasted the best coffee pretty much everywhere.

There was a simplicity to it, and he had come to appreciate the place. The fact that it had a view overlooking the ocean through the Nassau harbor was a plus too.

It was a reflex to head there, and enjoying the feel of the ocean breeze cutting through the streets put a smile on his face as he found his way to the small coffee shop.

"What can I get you, sir?" a tall, powerfully built man asked him as he found his way to one of the tables on the terrace of the house.

"Just a coffee, black, two sugars, please."

"Right away."

Kris settled in and enjoyed the view. As much as he hated the oppressive heat of the island, which the steady wind straight from the ocean made tolerable, it was hard to deny that the views in the area were to die for.

Or kill for. Kill was the preferred option.

He shook his head. It was the kind of thinking that came from another time, another mindset, and another life, one he'd hoped had been put away for good.

But no, someone wanted to drag him out and put him through his paces.

"Mr. Kringle?"

Kris looked up and turned to face the smaller man who stood over him just as the waiter returned with his coffee.

"Do I know you?" Kris asked, reaching for his wallet.

"Oh, don't bother. We've covered the bill for you. And no, you do not know me, but I've been told about you. Your appearance is...rather distinctive."

Sure enough, the coffee was placed in front of him with

no bill forthcoming. The waiter beat a hasty retreat as the intruder took a seat across from him.

"Manners say I should invite you to sit before you do so," Kris growled, taking a tentative sip of his coffee. He doubted anyone would go to the effort to poison him, but there was no being too careful.

"I assumed we could do away with such frivolities, considering I picked up your bill for the fantastic coffee you're drinking."

Kris leaned forward and inspected the man closely. Thinning blond hair, mostly hidden by a white fedora, a long, aquiline nose, and eyes that were a little too close together, which made the man look cross-eyed behind his horn-rimmed glasses.

He was short, thin, and wore expensive clothes, mostly white. Even his shoes were white. The man was desperately trying to look like a tourist in the region.

"I'm thinking a South African accent," Kris said, narrowing his eyes. "But you've started taking on hints of the local accent in your English too, which means you've been around here too long for you to just be a tourist. You've been here a while. Not a banker, not with that watch, so I'm going to go out on a limb and say that you call yourself a consultant, but all you really are is a middle-man. How close am I?"

The man's face twitched, but he brought it under control, quickly faking a smile. "You know, they said you're good. I'm glad to see you live up to your reputation."

"Said that about me, did they?" Kris took another sip of his coffee, now more confident that nobody was trying to kill him just yet. "I'm going to have to thank *them* for having so much faith in me. I'd really like to do the thanking in person."

"I'm sure your chance will come eventually, but I have been told that you are trying to get in touch with an insurance company regarding a vehicle you've misplaced. Their words, not mine, of course, and we both know what they mean by them."

"Right. What did this insurance company say about recovering my lost vehicle?"

"They said it is not a complete loss and that you should be able to find what you are searching for at the Dolphin Mall in Miami, Florida in two days' time. They said that you should meet them there if you wish to reclaim your vehicle, and they will provide you with their list of demands. They said that you will know who you are looking for because it will be like looking in a mirror. That one I cannot decipher for you since I cannot think there are many who look like you in the world. Again, I only repeat their words."

Kris nodded. "Thankfully, I know what they're talking about."

"Excellent. I am a simple lawyer in this paradise, doling out the instructions I received, as well as this phone, upon which they said you would receive further instructions on the day of the meeting. Enjoy your coffee, Mr. Kringle."

The man stood, placed the burner phone on the table, and beat a hasty retreat, not so much as looking back. At least his instincts were good. It was wise for middlemen to avoid overstaying their welcome. Contrary to popular belief, there was a benefit to shooting the proverbial messenger since the action sent a message all its own.

CHAPTER FOUR

The phone was rigged to only work in the continental US, meaning he would likely not have much time to get to Miami before the instructions started to arrive.

He made a quick stop at his parents' place to make sure his mother's chili was still the best in the world before it was time to schedule a flight from Nassau's international airport to Miami.

He wasn't used to having to use planes and go through airports anymore. The ability to slip from country to country without being spotted in a high-tech aircraft was one of the perks he had gotten accustomed to after taking up the mantle of St. Nick.

But now he was stuck traveling in a cramped aluminum tube. They didn't make the seats with a man his size in mind, meaning even the business class seat he'd paid for was just on the edge of uncomfortable.

At least it was a short flight. A few orders of orange juice from the stewardess and a couple of episodes of what he assumed was currently showing on television were all he had time to enjoy. There was a laugh track for the show, which was about a group of quirky individuals doing quirky things that likely would never happen in the real world.

It was distracting enough to make the flight go by a little quicker, and before he knew it, he was going through Customs.

"Anything to declare?" the bored-looking Customs agent asked him, not looking up from the passport.

"Nope."

"Welcome to Miami, sir."

He reclaimed his passport and headed through the winding hallways. He didn't even have a carry-on. Most of his stuff had been sent separately since airplane companies tended to disapprove of folk bringing firearms and other dangerous equipment on their planes.

All he could hope for was that everything would arrive in time for his meeting at the Dolphin Mall. Otherwise, he would be stuck with what he could get his hands on, which would leave him at a severe disadvantage.

He was already at a severe disadvantage, he thought, pausing and looking around the arrival hall, taking note of all the cameras that were converging on his location. Someone had gone through a lot of trouble to make sure he got this far in their little game, which meant he was required to be alive at this point.

That was an advantage. The downside was that he wouldn't know when their need for him to be alive would change.

Best to find them as quickly as possible.

"Mr. Kringle?"

Kris looked down at a young man in a bright orange uniform with the logo for a rental car agency emblazoned on the front.

"That's me," he answered. He needed to make himself look less conspicuous.

"I'm sorry, all that they sent was a photo and your name. I was told to find you and let you know we have a car waiting for you in the garage, rented by...Workshop Enterprises, LLC?"

Subtle.

"Well, lead the way, Kevin," Kris responded, picking up the kid's name from his tag.

The airport was a damn maze, even with the thousands of signs that had been put up all over the place, which meant they circled what felt like a dozen times at the very least. His mind was on how the Workshop might have been able to rent a car for him. The more likely explanation was that someone was yanking his chain.

There was only one possibility for the culprit, but Kris tried to keep an open mind as they entered the underground parking garage and headed to the area reserved for car rental agencies.

The lack of wind in Miami made the heat even more insufferable than it had been in the Bahamas. Kris had never thought it would come to this, but he was starting to miss the cooler—and icier—conditions in the North Pole, even during the winter.

Still, there was nothing for it. He would have to grit his teeth and get through it, with nothing on his mind but getting the job done.

"Here we are," Kevin said, pulling a key out of his

pocket. "I've always had a special place for the Ford Taurus in my heart. My dad was a cop back in the day when they were the standard for police cruisers. I mean, they have the new-ish Interceptors now, but you just don't get the same feel, you know?"

Kris did see the appeal, although probably not for the same reason that had the kid smiling as he filled out the paperwork required to turn the car over. Tauruses were metaphorically a dime a dozen in this country, especially the silver sedans. The car would not turn a single head, nondescript as it was, and the vehicle had a decent engine and wasn't too difficult to drive.

In the end, it was not the kind of car that generally made it into action movies, but it was one he preferred to have in his time of need, even if it wasn't the best-looking vehicle of all time.

"All set, Mr. Kringle," Kevin said as he offered him the form to sign. Kris did and moved toward the car, his brows furrowed as he approached the vehicle, eyeing it dubiously. He couldn't think of a way the Workshop could rent him a car in Miami of all places, but who the hell would profit from making sure he had adequate transportation?

Maybe someone who wanted to keep tabs on him, but at the same time, it would only take a minute or two to disable any tracking system that they might have planted.

As Kevin headed back to work, Kris took the time to inspect the vehicle, looking over every bit that he could see. There was nothing about it that would indicate it was a trap, and he finally beeped the lock and opened the driver's side door.

Still nothing. No explosions, no gas released. He was alive and feeling a little foolish about standing outside.

He climbed in, finding the seat a little more comfortable than he expected in a Ford Taurus. As he gripped the wheel, a screen rotated away from the dashboard. It was black for a few long seconds before turning blue, displaying no brand or logo before flicking over to a scanner.

"Fingerprint identity confirmed," it read. "Kris Kringle, St. Nicholas. Welcome."

He narrowed his eyes as the screen changed again, this time to a menu of choices. Weapons, scanners, accessories, defenses, and music were the available options.

After a moment of thought, he pressed the button for weapons. This was looking a lot more like the Workshop's work, but a few questions remained.

The glove compartment opened, showing him a pair of Glocks, with the options of a suppressor and different magazines for the weapon. As he inspected those, he could see another metal briefcase waiting for him, this one with a high-powered rifle inside in case he needed it.

"Okay," he muttered, looking around the car. "How long has this been one of the perks for Santa? Did my predecessor make any use of it, and what are the limits involved?"

He wasn't really surprised that there was no answer from the car, although he was maybe a little disappointed. If there was ever the opportunity for a dialogue to be opened, it was when the Workshop provided him with a damn spy car.

With a quick shake of his head, Kris pressed the button

to hide the weapons again. Best not to have them visible if he was pulled over by a local law enforcement officer. Not that he was expecting to be pulled over, but then he didn't need to think about how likely it was that it would happen.

A day passed, and Kris found himself entering the mindset that he wasn't very comfortable with anymore. Even so, it was a lot easier than he thought it would be, studying his surroundings, making sure that he knew all the ins and outs of the place. Like shaving his head, it was a way of mentally preparing for an operation.

He settled in for a dreamless sleep in a nearby hotel. It was the first time he hadn't had nightmares in the years since he started delivering presents from the North Pole.

He was up with the sun and took advantage of the hotel's free breakfast before heading out. He made sure he wasn't followed to the Dolphin Mall, circling the perimeter a few times before the place opened before finally making his way into the underground parking lot.

He wasn't surprised that the place was getting crowded this early in the morning. Three days before Christmas, there were going to be thousands of local parents desperate to make sure that their Christmas lists were filled.

It would provide him with much-needed cover, but he was entering a zone with cameras all over the place. That meant that if someone was expecting him to arrive, he wasn't going to find a way to approach them without being seen.

He put one of the pistols together with a suppressor, loaded it, and slipped it into the holster he had situated under his shoulder. The rifle would have to wait since there was no way he could carry it without drawing attention.

The place was filling up quickly, even though only a handful of stores were open. It looked like it was going to be a hectic shopping day for everyone involved. The cries of energized children fresh off of a sugar high from their breakfast cereals and pastries were the most identifiable of the sounds in the place.

He wasn't surprised to see a group of mall Santas setting schedules and getting ready for a busy day and the lines that would soon start forming.

Kris paused when one of them broke away from the group with no questions being asked and jogged over to where he was standing. He was in full costume, with the fake belly, beard, cap, and boots. It was a cheap imitation of the uniform Kris had back at the Workshop, but it would pass in the eyes of a child.

"You Kringle?" the mall Santa asked, coming to a halt in front of him. The man's skin was well-tanned, with dark eyes and a few scars, mostly hidden behind the fake beard.

"Sounds like it." Kris studied the man for clues about what he could expect from him if push came to shove, but the costume hid most of it. He was tall, and the boots were not just for show. He was a mercenary of some kind, the type who could easily handle a combat situation if he needed to. "Not really my reflection, though."

"Enough of it for the point to be made," the merc rebutted, motioning with his head. "Come on. We've got work to do. No funny business."

Kris followed the man through the mall, and he could feel eyes following them through the whole building. Kris' beard was enough to make him look like he might be applying for the position, so the assumption would be that he was a new guy getting set up for the work that would be coming their way.

Seasonal work, but still.

They came to a halt in front of one of the service-only doors, and the Santa swiped a card through a reader and looked up at one of the nearby cameras before the door clicked open.

Kris could almost feel the eyes on the back of his head as he slipped through it.

"All right, I got to do this," the man said, motioning for Kris to raise his hands, which he did without question. The man's hands worked with the quick, practiced motions to search him, quickly finding the weapon tucked under his arm.

"Wasn't told to come unarmed," Kris explained as the weapon was placed aside.

The merc didn't answer, just finished the search before heading to a corner of the storage room that they were in, where a computer with an interesting and unusual set of controls was waiting for him on a desk.

"They want you to put in the controls," the merc said simply, motioning for him to keep heading toward the corner.

Kris could see a weapon inside the man's red jacket, which he had opened to make sure the firearm was in easy reach. That was a hint that he was expecting trouble from Kris, but the lack of cameras in the room meant they didn't need to keep an eye on what was happening.

To Kris' mind, that meant only one thing. He had walked into his execution.

He moved slowly and deliberately, looking around the room again while trying not to be obvious about it.

Too much was wrong with what he was seeing. If they were going to kill him, why did they need him to input some controls into a computer? Why did they want him to go through this whole charade? Why not gun him down in the Bahamas and pay the cops off?

His eyes fell on the controls, and he put his hands on them. It felt a little too natural, although he needed a few seconds to realize why. They were exact copies of the controls for his sleigh, complete with the fingerprint readers and biometric scanners that were supposed to keep anyone but him from being able to drive it.

That made things a lot clearer. This whole thing wasn't about him. It was about his sleigh.

He narrowed his eyes.

"Is there a problem?" the merc asked, taking a step closer.

"I...don't know what I'm looking at," Kris lied, tapping the controls. "I mean, what am I supposed to do here? Is this some sort of game, like an escape-room riddle?"

It was clear the merc had no idea what he was doing there either. He craned his neck around to see what was going on while pressing his finger to his ear, keeping one hand close to the weapon inside his red jacket.

Just a little closer.

"I...what are you saying?" the merc asked, clearly speaking to the people on the other side of his earpiece. "The reception in here is a fucking nightmare. Just let me..."

He was inching forward, anticipating that something would go wrong and trying to be as on top of things as he could.

Close enough.

Kris snapped around at the hips, using his elbow to hook the man's hand away from his coat. The merc sucked in a deep breath, his body reacting to the sudden combat conditions that he was encountering as Kris twisted around, locking the man's right arm with his left and reaching up to catch the left arm with his right. He took the opportunity to crash a closed fist into the man's nose before pushing him into the closest wall.

"Son of a bi—"

The man's cursing was interrupted by Kris' knee crunching into his ribs. Kris could feel his heart rate increasing, but not by much as he kept a grip on the fake Santa, staying calm as he brought his knee into the man's unprotected midsection again. This time the cracked ribs broke, knocking the man's breath out of his lungs in a rush.

It felt a little too casual, too comfortable. Kris knew that he was out of shape. His body wasn't reacting the way he wanted it to, but that still put him leagues above the skill of the man in front of him.

Kris formed his right hand into a spear as he released the merc's left hand. His own left crossed and pushed the man a little to the side, and Kris hooked his right hand behind the merc just below his broken ribs.

A pained grunt told him he'd hit the merc's kidney, even though the padding around his stomach provided some protection. The man screamed and dropped to his knees to recover from the onslaught of pain coursing through his body.

The next series of motions came a little too naturally. Kris gripped the back of the merc's head and dragged it into the path of his rising knee. No crunch this time, but the man's eyes rolled back, and he hit the hard concrete without so much as a flinch.

He knew he should end the merc's life, but Kris hesitated even as he peeled the man's Santa suit off and collected his weapon. Things had changed. Killing was not off the table, morally speaking, but there was no point in murdering the unconscious merc, not that he was an innocent man.

Hell, if Kris killed him, there would likely be a lot of people who lived longer because the man wouldn't kill *them*, but he couldn't bring himself to do it.

Kris scowled and got into the costume. It was thankfully within range of his size, although the shoulders were a little tight. He appropriated the man's earpiece and pressed it into his own ear.

Not the most hygienic of solutions, but he was short on time.

"Vic? Vic, are you still there?"

As much as he wanted to, he didn't reply. He pulled a dongle out of his pocket and slipped it into the computer. There was a chance that it was transmitting information to where he could find the new sleigh, and he needed to make sure that worked out.

"Vic, pick up," the voice said again before growling, "Greg, head in there and check on him."

The dongle clicked, telling him a connection was established, and he tucked the man's weapon into his shoulder holster before returning to where his Glock was waiting for him.

It would be interesting to find out where the transmission was coming from, but for now, he needed to get out of the mall.

More mercs were coming. Kris checked his weapon, making sure it was ready to fire before moving toward the door.

He expected to feel something—a hint of exhilaration, maybe some fear, but nothing rose to the fore. Like any other day of waking up, making himself breakfast, and heading to his office for a few hours of checking the lists before taking time off for his daily workout. Just another day.

He couldn't tell if that was a bad thing.

CHAPTER FIVE

Miami's malls were as much of a maze as their airport. Kris kept his weapon out of sight as he looked around the place, waiting for the rest of the mercs to show up. For a moment, he wondered why they weren't converging on him, but then he remembered the groups of shoppers filling the mall. Kris realized they were slowed down by the crowds and because they were technically working in the Dolphin Mall as their Santas.

Still, it wouldn't last, and Kris grew more anxious every second that none of the men approached him.

Then one of them did.

The man froze in place, and Kris detected a hint of hesitation. The crew was not familiar with each other, and they were all wearing disguises, which meant he couldn't be sure if the man in front of him was their target or one of his comrades.

Kris took advantage of the pause. He broke into a jog and approached the man while keeping his head on a swivel like the mall Santa was not a threat.

The hesitation continued.

"Did you see Greg?" Kris asked, keeping his hand on the weapon hidden inside his jacket. "Dumbass was supposed to be checking on Vic."

"I...no."

"Shit. Do you think that Kringle guy killed Vic?"

"I told those assholes not to send Vic in there alone, but they said they couldn't trust—"

The moment the merc looked away, Kris drew his weapon and pulled the trigger—a double-tap to the man's chest and a confirmation shot to the head, just to be sure, all before the merc even started to drop. The subsonic rounds were softer than the alternative, but the crack was still distinctive enough that a group of shoppers shouted, looking around. Kris had already tucked the weapon back into his jacket and was moving away from the dead Santa.

They were talking about a busted light or someone lighting firecrackers inside the mall. A few were laughing about how startled they had been.

He counted fifteen seconds before anyone saw the dead man.

The screams would warn him well in advance of the sirens. He wasn't worried about the mall's security staff, although he didn't want to injure any of them for doing their job. All he needed to do was get out of the mall and get to his car and away from this place before more problems came up.

Too many things would go wrong if he stuck around.

The escalator was as far as he got before he heard the cracks of suppressed weapons being fired behind him. Kris ducked, then looked around and saw three men in Santa outfits rushing toward him. The only thing that saved his life was how inaccurate their weapons were at that distance.

He didn't shoot back. They weren't worried about hitting nearby shoppers, but he was. And he could already hear the screams echoing around the mall, telling him that the dead Santa had been found.

Kris stayed below the aluminum walls of the escalator, which gave him some cover, although it would run out quickly.

He drew his weapon and pointed it up the steps as he watched and waited until movement appeared on the escalator.

The bright red suits made it easy to tell they weren't random locals caught in the crossfire. The first of the three mercs fell, clutching a pair of wounds to his right leg. Kris had been aiming for the torso, but wounding them was as good as killing at this point.

The other two skidded to a halt before they were caught by the other three bullets he fired in their direction, not bothering to pull their wounded comrade out of the line of fire.

The escalator was slow-moving and had a long way to go to the ground floor. One of the men peeked out from around the corner, trying to judge the distance.

He collapsed, the contents of his skull splattering behind him as one of the two rounds Kris fired struck.

Damn suppressor would be the death of him.

Kris drew the magazine out, not bothering to check how close to empty it was before slapping another one in.

The third and last of the mercs was smarter. He

smoothly vaulted over the edge and climbed to the outside of the escalator, then slid down while keeping his grip on the railing. He wasn't going to be able to shoot while moving down, but he would reach the bottom before Kris did.

It would give him the advantage, especially if he jumped down the moment it was safe to do so.

Kris hated desperate times. The desperate measures that always resulted were a pain in the ass to live with.

Keeping low, he moved up the steps as quickly as he could, fighting the downward trajectory of the escalator. He wouldn't have a clean shot on the bastard coming down, and any shot that didn't hit him could end up wounding or killing an innocent bystander.

He watched the hands on the rail come down to meet him, timing the encounter in his head before jumping over the guard wall.

The mall Santa's eyes widened when he saw Kris coming for him. The impact knocked the man from his perch, and Kris gripped his chest and the padding around his waist to make sure he was underneath as they fell.

It was about fifteen feet, and Kris' breath was knocked out of him when they landed. Still, he had some extra padding of his own, not to mention the merc to break his fall. It wasn't high enough to kill, but it was enough to daze the man and maybe give him some back problems.

Kris pressed his weapon into the man's chest, pulled the trigger, and watched the life drain from the eyes of another mall Santa.

"Well, if that isn't fucking ominous," Kris whispered,

pushing up as gingerly as he could manage before turning around.

In doing so, he realized that his action had not been as unseen as he'd hoped it would be. There was a young boy standing across from him. His black hair looked like it was growing out, and his clothes were in decent shape if showing a few wrinkles. His dark eyes were wide and his mouth was open since he was holding a half-eaten churro a few inches away from it, the powdered sugar and cinnamon making a mess on his shirt.

Kris straightened and reached into the pocket of the Santa suit, where he could feel a few candy canes.

He pulled out three and handed them to the boy, who took them without breaking from the shocked expression and frozen body.

"Probably best not to tell your folks about this," Kris said as the boy took the candy canes. "Run along now. Find them."

The boy nodded and pocketed the candy before turning around and running away. Kris scowled and shook his head. Innocent victims weren't only those who were hit by bullets. The kid would likely need a few months of therapy to get over seeing Santa killing Santa.

He would think about that later. He checked his weapon again and tucked it into his coat while running toward the signs that pointed to the underground parking lot. There would be no fighting until he got there, he realized, since screams were starting to echo around the whole mall as the other bodies were found.

The police would be coming in short order. Places like this always had patrol cars in the vicinity.

"We need to pull out," someone growled over the earbud comm. "The cops are going to be here in three minutes."

"Not until we have Kringle," the leader of the operation snapped back. "He's heading to the garage. You need to be waiting for him. Also, I think he's on our channel. Switch to another frequency."

"That lasted longer than I thought it would," Kris muttered, pulling the bud from his ear and tossing it into a nearby trash can as he headed into the garage.

There were enough of them waiting in the parking lot to make him pause and check his ammo before going any farther.

His phone buzzed as he did, and the lights of the Taurus blinked a few times to remind him it was there and more than capable of coming to his aid.

Which was for the best, really. He only had the two magazines, and neither was full.

"Where the hell is he?" one of the Santas shouted.

Not the most professional bunch, these guys. That was the only reason he was still alive. Still, he counted six of them in the garage, all armed with suppressed pistols, meaning they would have about the same effective range.

Maybe another exit.

No, there were more waiting upstairs, and more potential collateral damage if he got into a protracted firefight. Not an option.

"Straight into the deep end it is, then," Kris whispered, pressing a button on his phone before stepping out from behind his cover. He gripped his pistol with both hands as he moved toward one of the nearby pillars while pulling the trigger.

The gunfire was difficult to pin down as he advanced on them. One of the group fell back, gripping his chest, while the rest finally managed to find Kris, just in time for him to step behind the pillar.

"That's one," Kris whispered, ejecting the empty magazine and pulling the other one out, checking to see how many rounds he still had.

"Six," he whispered. "Plus sixteen in the one Vic gave me. Nice of him. I mean, he wasn't going to use it anyway, but it was still a nice gesture. I don't feel bad about leaving him alive."

He pulled his phone out and checked the cameras in the headlights, making himself as small as possible while rounds chipped off the concrete of the pillar he was behind. They were circling to try to flank him from both sides; that much was clear from the cameras on the car, but he could make things a little better.

The car had defenses that would escalate things. It pulled out, following the road and circling around to where the larger of the two groups was standing, trying to advance on him as two more laid down cover fire.

"Did someone order a little Christmas spirit?" Kris asked with a small grin, flashing the lights again and this time revving the engine as he sent it quickly toward the group. Two managed to dive out of the way, but one of them was caught by the vehicle.

It knocked him over, and the other two shooters turned their attention to the car.

An opening if Kris was ever going to get one. He kept

low and opened fire on the two who were providing cover for the others.

One of them fell back as a round cut into his throat, but the other dived behind a pillar before Kris could fire at him.

He dropped the empty pistol and smoothly charged toward the remaining three, who were confused by the car that was attacking them without anyone driving it.

Best to keep them on their toes. He grabbed the first one by the head and smashed it into a nearby car window hard enough to break the glass as he vaulted over the one that had been run over.

The third got a shot off, but the round went a little high, smashing into one of the lights and sending sparks flying all over before Kris hit him.

His time spent playing defensive end however many years ago during high school came to his aid. The tackle knocked the breath out of the merc's chest and drove him back into another pillar with enough force that he ended up hammering his head into the concrete. The splat was audible, and the merc left behind a red stain as he sank to the floor, unconscious.

Kris pulled Vic's pistol from inside his coat, holding it with both hands as he finished off the dazed man on the ground with a quick shot to the head.

The other two were unconscious or dead, and Kris moved toward the one man remaining in the garage with him.

He narrowed his eyes as the merc ran away, not bothering to stay under cover or shoot back.

The weapon in his hand kicked three times. The first

round went high, but the other two found their target, cutting into his back and punching through. He staggered and dropped to the floor of the garage.

His ears were ringing, but given the sirens he could hear outside, he was not going to get out of the complex, not on his own.

"Shit," he hissed, moving to the car that was waiting for him. He pulled the door open and hid the two pistols he had used inside. It didn't look like there were any cameras in the area, and Kris made sure the car headed back to the spot it had been parked in as he went back toward the mall. He could hear the police starting to make their rounds.

He was interested in finding out if, given that there would be dozens of police showing up, the mercs would get into a fight with them. When he returned to the mall, there was a lot less fighting than he'd thought there would be.

The mercs had beat a hasty retreat, taking their wounded but leaving the bodies. They were likely wiping the security footage too.

It would protect them, but they were going to end up protecting him too. Small miracles.

"You!"

Kris tried not to snap around like he was expecting a fight. He wasn't going to allow himself to be arrested, although injuring the local police wasn't an option either. He needed to find another way out.

His eyebrows shot up when he realized it was a man in a suit with graying hair and glasses. Not the look he would expect from the local cops.

"Me?" Kris asked.

"Yeah, you! Are you kidding? All the other Santas disappear, ended up getting shot or caught up with the cops. If you're none of the above, I need someone to man the stations on the third floor. We've got a line going out my fudging wazoo there, and someone needs to take up the role."

Well, that was one way to keep himself above suspicion.

"They were shooting, and there was shouting..." Kris began as the man took his arm.

"I don't give a...holy shit, you're a lot harder under the suit! No, never mind, no time! I need you on that fudging seat, listening to the gosh-darn kids!"

Kris imagined that there was a no-cursing rule at the man's home, or maybe in the corporate office. He followed suit, letting himself be led up to the third floor, where, sure enough, there was a long line of excited kids with bored parents waiting for him.

He'd never imagined the work would result in him pretending to be Santa in a mall, but Kris couldn't help but smile at what he supposed was irony as he took the seat. One of the teenagers dressed as elves unhooked the red rope keeping the kids out and motioned for the first to come through.

He had never thought of himself as a child person. The names on the lists had always been distant and foreign to him. Meeting the kids in person was considerably more involved, and the first kid, maybe three years old with bright red hair, wearing a bright blue shirt with a superhero's face on it, seemed like just the sort to start his day off.

"Hi, Santa!" the kid shouted, clambering into his lap as

the parents laughed tiredly. "Wow, is your beard real? The other Santa's beard fell off when I pulled on it."

Kris winced as the kid tried the same thing with him, but he waved the parents off when they stepped in to try to stop the little one.

"Just because the beard comes off, it doesn't mean the spirit of Santa isn't there," Kris said, smiling when the kid finally let his beard go. "What's your name, little one? No, wait, it's James, isn't it?"

A simple trick of looking at the name on the tag.

"Yes! How did you know?"

"Because I've made a list and checked it twice to make sure you've been nice. So, what can I get you for Christmas?"

"I want one of the new iPads and a Captain America action figure. Oh, oh, and my friend has the newest Fort-nite skin!"

"I'm sure you'll get exactly what you've been wanting," Kris noted, motioning to get the kid's attention directed at the camera for their picture.

It was a long line, but the names and the faces didn't fade into a blur as he'd expected them to. Even when the elves went on their lunch break, he stayed on.

"You're up next," he heard the manager say, and another Santa entered the back of the magical kingdom, or what-ever it was called.

It gave him the chance to see one more of the kids, who shuffled over the carpet to where Kris was sitting.

"What's your name, kiddo?" Kris asked the young boy. He was about five, with curly black hair that refused to be contained by the single elastic.

"William. My friends call me Bill."

"What can I get for you this Christmas?"

The boy looked around and shook his head. "Mom and Dad already got me what I wanted, but they couldn't buy the headphones my sister Amy wanted for when she goes to the doctor every Friday. She keeps saying she needs them to be soundproof, but she never says why."

Kris could see the manager gesturing to him from behind a curtain, but he ignored the man for the moment.

"You know, kid, I think she'll get what she wants this Christmas."

His dark eyes brightened. "Thanks, Santa!"

He was ready to jump off before the picture was taken, but his parents contained him, allowing Kris to exit as his replacement was quickly ushered in.

"Nice work..."

"Kris," he informed the man.

"Right, Kris, great work. And I really appreciate you working through your lunch break. Get with Jill at HR, and she'll have a check for you."

He'd worked through his lunch break, apparently. Kris checked his watch and realized it was almost four in the afternoon.

"Oh, right. No problem. Thanks for having me."

He pulled the costume off and placed it in the bin where employees were supposed to put their clothes to be washed after a shift, then pivoted and headed toward the garage where his car was parked.

CHAPTER SIX

The screen was coming on by the time that he climbed into the driver's seat, but he didn't pause to look at it until they were out of the mall and heading away from where he could still see a handful of police vehicles hanging around.

"I'd just love to see the spin they put on the story," Kris whispered. "Maybe they'll put it down as gangland violence or something. Criminals dressed as mall Santas shoot up mall is the kind of headline that writes itself."

Not that he was going to hang around long enough for it to be published. The screen showed the trace he'd put on the computer. It had been hours, and the trace had long since been completed, showing him a building in Manhattan.

"Been a while since I've visited good old NYC," he said, looking around the car. "You know, it wouldn't kill you to put a word in here or there. People are going to think the old dumbass with the white beard is fucking nuts."

There was no answer from the Workshop, but his

phone did buzz in his pocket, indicating an alert coming through on the car's Bluetooth connection.

Tickets had been bought to take him to JFK in less than three hours, along with a ticket for him to collect yet another vehicle waiting for him once he got there. He assumed it was going to be another nondescript vehicle that allowed him to drive around the area with no issues about being seen.

If he was equipped again as he had been in Miami, he was going to need to find a way to get a present for the Workshop. It was supporting him better than he had ever been supported in the past. Of course, he'd had no problem supporting himself—living and surviving on his wits.

But having the Workshop there to sustain him in the field was definitely a plus. The Workshop's support was going to bring up a few questions about what was happening around him, but those would all have to wait until he had the sleigh back.

Delivering the car back to the rental agency felt wrong, considering how much he wanted to keep it, but driving all the way to New York would waste too much time. Hopefully the one he got his hands on in the city that never slept would be just as good.

It was quick work to check in again since he had no luggage, meaning he had a little while to get something to eat before boarding.

The truest sign that he was starting to get old presented itself when Kris found himself napping during the two and change hours he spent on the plane. He needed to be nudged by the stewardess to tell him they had landed.

There was no reason for him to feel better about being in New York than in Miami. The place was a hell of a lot more hectic, and the airport was packed with people since the holiday was coming up.

There were people from out of town who were visiting New York and denizens of the city who wanted to leave. It was an interesting combination.

Kris assumed the reason he felt more comfortable in the city was that it was snowing outside. As he picked up the new car, which was furnished with the same gadgets the other had been fitted with, even though it was a dark-blue Camry, he looked outside. The snow was coming down in sheets, and he couldn't feel more comfortable about the idea of driving through it.

It was slow going, but Kris filled the time by inspecting the location the signal had been traced to. It was a sloppy move on their part, but he was getting the feeling that they had been in a bit of a rush and had to grab low-level mercs to deal with him instead of bringing in professionals.

Still, their mistakes were his profit, and Kris studied the building to make sure it was what he was looking for. On the surface, there was nothing to set it apart from thousands of other office buildings that created the Manhattan skyline, but a closer look revealed the cracks. The first five floors had ten different corporate offices for small companies, but the sixth floor was separated from the rest of the building. It featured security checks and a very vague description of what the company that owned the other ten floors of the building did.

In his experience, all those pieces coming together

could only mean one thing: a security contractor, usually for the DOD, although they might work for one of the other three-letter agencies in the country.

It wasn't like them to be in a rush about operations, but then, maybe there was some sort of time crunch he wasn't aware of. He still didn't know why they had stolen the sleigh from him. All he knew was that the connection had been established when he touched the controls. As long as he could recover it, no more questions need be asked.

"I don't suppose you can get me intel on the group that owns the building?" Kris asked, then waited for but did not expect an answer from the car as traffic slowed to a crawl behind what appeared to be a minor accident. "No? Okay, I'll just have to do the research myself."

The only thing he could do was look into the buildings around it. Thankfully, as appeared to be the case with most business-heavy areas of Manhattan, there was a hotel directly across the street. Not the nicest of places from the looks of things, but it was the only option available if he was going to put himself as close to the building as possible without breaking the law.

It was a simple thing to book a room there for a few nights, as well as programming Waze to get him there through the lightest traffic.

Once he reached the island there wasn't much of it, allowing him to make better time. It wasn't long before he pulled his vehicle into the hotel's underground parking garage.

He collected the briefcase and the weapons from their hidden spot in the glove compartment but narrowed his eyes as the button to open the trunk started glowing a faint red.

There was no choice but to press the button, opening the trunk. He headed around the back to see what was waiting for him.

Kris was not surprised to find a small suitcase waiting for him with a note on top.

You can't ever be too prepared.

It looked like the elves had written it. Maybe they did know he was facing trouble and wanted to help. The suitcase was heavy enough to contain pretty much anything, but he wouldn't be opening it where there were likely to be cameras.

After locking the car, Kris headed into the reception area. He saw more than a few men in mid-range suits and coats standing around, either sipping coffee or drinking at the hotel bar, likely while waiting to leave or be checked in.

It was late enough at night for most of the check-ins to have been performed, but Kris wasn't going to worry about it. More than a few eyes turned to him as he moved through the room dressed as he was, looking the way he did. Most of the locals were businessmen, visiting from out of town, and Kris, with his long white beard, burly build, and less-than-formal wear, stood out like a sore thumb.

The receptionist offered a hint of a double-take before plastering a practiced smile on her face.

"Good evening, sir. How can I help you?"

"I've got a reservation," he answered, pulling his phone out and showing her the email he'd gotten to confirm his reservation. "Kris Kringle."

"Kris?"

He turned around and saw a woman standing behind him. She was short, only coming up to his chest in the four-inch heels she was wearing. Her blonde hair was pulled into a tight bun, matching her rimless glasses and steel-gray pantsuit. Her attire and demeanor gave him and anyone else the impression of a no-nonsense business-woman who didn't mind showcasing her attractiveness in a formal setting.

Of course, he did recognize her, just as she had him, although he guessed her job of recognizing him was considerably easier.

"Claudia?" Kris asked as though there was any doubt in his mind. "Fancy meeting you here."

She laughed, moving to hug him awkwardly. "Yeah, fancy that. I thought you were still up north."

He narrowed his eyes. She hadn't taken the news that he was leaving his profitable job in order to be Santa Claus very well, calling him delusional and leaving him via an email after she had caught a plane to New York once it was clear that his mind was made up. It had been a few years since that fateful conversation between the two of them.

"I've got some stuff to do around here," Kris said, keeping his answer intentionally vague. They had met on the job, and she had been responsible for sending a lot of work his way once she went corporate. She was as sharp as nails and would know if he was lying about anything. Best to keep her out of the loop.

She looked at his shaved head and narrowed her eyes, tilting her head. "You're looking good. Not wearing that ridiculous red costume anymore. Does this mean that your delusional episode is finished?"

He instinctively ran his fingers over his shaved head and shook his head. "Just here taking care of some personal stuff is all."

"Right. You working again?"

She wasn't going to let it go. Kris smiled as the receptionist handed him his room key card, saying it was on the twelfth floor.

"Just taking care of some personal stuff," he said again, deflecting. It was fairly obvious, but she would know that even if he was working again, he wouldn't be able to talk about it with her.

"Okay, I can respect that," Claudia replied, following him as he made his way to the elevator with his luggage. "Let me know if you have some time while you're in town. Maybe we can get a quick drink or something and catch up."

"Sounds good." Kris kept the fake smile in place as she handed him her card. The elevator door dinged, and he stepped inside. "See you around, Claudia."

"See ya."

The smile stayed in place as he watched the elevator doors shut. When he finally relaxed his features, he looked down at the card she'd given him. Chief Operations Officer was a step up from her past position as a consultant. Claudia always had been a cold, calculating person, and the fact that he'd thought she was on his side right until she wasn't had cut deeper than he was willing to admit.

He shook his head and ripped the card into quarters as the doors opened again, then dragged his luggage out of the elevator and headed toward his room.

He paused briefly next to a housekeeping cart to toss the remains of the torn-up card.

The request to have a room on the north side of the building had been honored, and Kris pulled the blinds up to look across the street at the building he had in his sights.

"Time to get to work," he whispered.

CHAPTER SEVEN

There was only so much research he could do before it started to tell on him. Kris took a deep breath and leaned back in his seat next to the window, rubbing his eyes and trying to think of something else for a second.

A lot of the night had been spent taking a look at the place. He could only see so much from this side, which meant a few hours were needed to request the building plans online.

There were certain facts he couldn't ignore at this point. The signal was still coming from the building, which meant his sleigh was probably still there.

It had to be. It was the afternoon of December twenty-third, which gave him precisely one day to find the vehicle, recover it, and head to the North Pole to get back on track to complete the work expected of him during the holiday.

Not the timing that he had hoped for, but those were the breaks. He needed to get the job done.

Maybe that was why he had been picked for the job. It couldn't have been that he was the best person to make sure the presents were delivered on time. Maybe someone had seen a situation like this on the horizon and known he was the one who could make the recovery in time.

"No pressure, then," he whispered, looking through his binoculars again and picking up on the security people wandering through the building across the street from him.

He could see what looked like weapons labs in the area, although they appeared to be testing the results through simulations on massive computers and servers housed on the tenth floor. Coincidentally, that also appeared to be where most of the security was housed.

That was a boon. Kris had no intention of stealing corporate secrets, and the floor was too heavily packed with computers, servers, and the cooling system required to keep both operational for his sleigh to be there.

No, the most likely location for the sleigh was the roof, where he saw a good amount of security as well, but less than on the tenth floor. From the looks of it, the rest of the staff would need a solid minute to get up to the roof.

Which left six men to hold it on their own. Getting in from below was not going to be an option. The hotel was a decent spot to get access from, however. It was ten floors higher than the other building, which meant getting over on a wire was feasible, although for whatever reason, he couldn't see the sleigh from the roof.

Thankfully, the suitcase in his car's trunk had been equipped with an air gun that could launch the grappling hook and its hundred and fifty yards of high-tensile-strength steel wire across with no difficulty. There was also body armor, along with flashbangs and smoke grenades, which would be necessary to breach. They would slightly improve his chances of surviving, and any advantage would be accepted with many thanks.

"No real need to plan this sort of thing," Kris muttered to himself as he kept looking through the binoculars. "Need to be loose. Get in and out as quickly as possible."

Unfortunately, it seemed as though his only escape route was using the sleigh.

That would put him in a lot of danger potentially for nothing, especially if this was a trap. It might have been easy to track them this quickly because they wanted him to find them.

That being the case, he still needed to head in. He didn't have time to shop around for another plan. Sure, a proper operation would increase his chances of success and survival, but that would take a couple of months to plan, get the right team together, and account for as many of the variables as he could.

Less than a day to prepare for the operation meant that he had to leave a lot of room for improvisation. Night was going to be the best time to go in, after six, which was when their crew was reduced to the barest bones on patrol.

He had a way in, and a time, and a place. All that was left to do was get his equipment together. Kris stood and moved over to the bed, where he had put his suppressed Glock together, as well as the P90 that had been in the car. Not his favorite submachine gun, but he appreciated the increased firepower since he was heading into an unfamiliar situation where he was facing an unknown number of hostiles on their turf.

His body armor went on first, and he had just finished

strapping it on and covering it with a coat when he heard footsteps outside the door.

Heavy boots, shuffling and moving around close to the door. Kris didn't need to think about it; he collected his pistol and moved to the door when he heard someone knock on it.

"Yeah?" he called, looking through the peephole.

Four men were dressed in what would pass for the uniform most of the hotel workers wore, offset by the combat boots on their feet.

"Housekeeping!" one of the men called, looking around and shrugging awkwardly as his three comrades eyed him.

"Okay, I'm coming," Kris answered, pressing the barrel of his Glock to the door and aiming at what he could see in the peephole. "More than once a year, apparently."

"Pardon?"

It was probably best they hadn't heard. He pulled the trigger, and the pistol kicked in his hand as a deafening crack filled the room. It was probably not loud enough to be heard in the surrounding rooms.

The merc closest to the door never had a chance. He took a pair of rounds in the neck before he realized that he was being shot at.

Kris moved away from the door as the others reached for their weapons, immediately dropping their disguises and opening fire on the door.

He was already on the floor, and he pressed against the wall as they emptied the magazines of their Uzis through the door, leaving very little wood for them to deal with once they were finished. Kris heard them reloading and took a deep breath to keep from charging out then and there.

These mercs were probably of a higher caliber than those he'd faced in Miami. They would probably be expecting him to charge them while they were reloading and were ready for it.

No, best to wait and bide his time. They were coming in, after all.

The first man kicked his way through the mangled door, struggling a bit with the area around his head just as Kris moved forward, keeping himself low. A firm kick to the side of the merc's knee had it bending the wrong way with a loud pop and a crack as the man screamed. Kris grabbed him by the neck and wrenched him around, mostly blocking the doorway and dragging him down at the same time.

Thus shielded, Kris shoved his Glock around the merc who was falling with him and opened fire on the mercs behind him.

The first one to fall gripped his chest and let out a gasp, but there was no indication the bullets had hit flesh or bone. They were wearing body armor, so body shots were out.

The man who was protecting him fought back even as his comrades peppered his back with bullets. The bullets did not pierce his armor, but they knocked the breath out of him. He pulled the man close, turning his weapon on the trio that was trying to break through. One fell back, two of the rounds punching through his head. Even with the suppressor on, this was like shooting fish in a barrel.

The one who remained dropped behind the cover of the walls, looking to reload and regroup.

After taking a moment to make sure he wasn't in danger, Kris turned his weapon on the merc groaning next to him and finished him off with a shot to the temple. He then rolled both of them over to the bed, where he reached up and grabbed one of the flashbangs he had laid out for the operation.

"No coal for you guys," Kris hissed, pulling the pin and throwing it out into the hallway. "Santa has upgraded to flashbangs!"

His warning came too late, and though he covered his ears, the stun grenade left his ears ringing. Probably not as bad as it was for the one in the hallway, but still.

He moved out, picking off the last one, still blinded and stunned, with a pair of headshots. Kris checked the hall to make sure there weren't any more coming after him before checking the contents of his mag. Almost empty.

He'd survived, but that was where the good news ended. Someone had sent a team for him, which meant they knew where he was. That meant the mission was blown.

Under any other circumstances, he would call the op off, take a step back, and look at it through another lens. Maybe even find another way in. But that wasn't an option here. The police would be getting calls, and the people who'd sent the mercs were more than likely aware that he had survived the attack.

He couldn't back down, not now, which meant he would charge head-first into a trap when they knew he was coming.

"This isn't going to be easy," he whispered to himself, quickly collecting his equipment and anything he couldn't leave behind for the police to find before sprinting to the stairwell.

It was the quickest way to the roof. His physical condition was as good as it had been when he was in his early thirties, but he was sucking in deep breaths once he reached the top of the stairs, keeping himself moving through the burn he could feel in his thighs as he pushed the door to the roof open.

The cold air smacked him in the face, reminding him that it was winter. The flash of red and blue lights told him the police had arrived, which pushed him to move faster as he connected one side of the wire to a secure spot on the roof before pulling out the grappling gun and aiming it at the building across the street.

Kris might have been worried about picking the wrong building if he hadn't spent the past ten hours staring at it. Even in the dark with the snow coming down, there was no way he could miss the spot.

He took a deep breath, looked down the sights of the grappling gun, and aimed at a spot where it would bury itself and sustain his weight as he crossed the street to the roof on the other side.

The hook whooshed as he released it. He watched as his shot flew true, give or take a few yards thanks to the gusting wind, and slammed into an elevated spot on the roof. The grappling gun quickly retracted to make sure the line was secure and taut.

Once it was in place, Kris worked quickly, clipping himself to the taut line with a carabiner that connected to his belt. He had no time to think or pause as he sprinted for the edge of the hotel roof.

This was the sort of thing he found himself missing—jumping off a building and feeling that twinge of doubt as to whether the line would hold him as he started zipping across the street, picking up speed until he needed to use the line's brakes.

Suddenly, Kris narrowed his eyes. A group moved out onto the roof and scanned around until they spotted him. They were carrying submachine guns like the other mercs, and they started shooting.

Their aim was off, but one quickly turned his attention to the line, pulling a knife out and starting to saw on it.

It wouldn't take long to get through it, and it was a long drop to the street below. Kris twisted on the line, releasing the brakes and speeding up while drawing his pistol and picking a window one floor down from the roof. He opened fire.

Three bullets punched through the window, and the fourth left it weak enough for what he needed. He looked up at the man who was furiously cutting the line, feeling every yank and tug. He held on for as long as he dared before hitting the quick release on his belt.

Very few feelings matched that sudden release and the drop through the air with nothing holding him back. He really should pack a parachute or a wing in case something like this happened again.

That was the last thought that came into his mind as he crashed into the hard glass feet-first. He went straight through and collided with something hard and unmoving on the other side, and everything went black.

CHAPTER EIGHT

"He's a lot better equipped than I thought he'd be."

"How well-equipped did you think Santa Claus would be, exactly?"

"I don't know, but not with a bullpup P90. Grappling line, smoke grenades, flashbangs. A Glock 17 with a suppressor. This guy's packing enough to besiege Quebec, and we don't have any intel on him except that he flies around the world once a year and gives kids presents?"

Kris felt hands dragging him, as well as the icy touch of the wind from outside. That meant he hadn't been unconscious for long. No point in letting them know he was awake, though.

They pulled him up onto a chair and secured his hands behind the back.

"You know what that means, right?"

"What?"

"That he used to be an operative. The intel we used to have on him was scrubbed in case some senator decided to check on what their contract money was being spent on."

"No shit? That explains the tats and him being built like a fucking athlete. I guess all that talk about the bowl full of jelly is a bowl full of shit."

"The fat Santa stereotype was propaganda put out back in the 20s and 30s, dude. Back before we had intel on the dude working out of the North Pole."

"Shut up, idiots," a woman's voice cut in. "He's awake and listening to everything you're saying."

A familiar voice. Kris opened his eyes, groaning when moving his neck was a little more painful than he'd expected it to be. There was no sign of a break or a herniated disk, though. Nothing that would keep him from moving. The same could be said of the rest of his body, although his right ankle felt like it wouldn't be at a hundred percent if he needed to do any running.

Going through the window had done a number on him, but it could have gone a lot worse, all things considered. There were four other people in the room. Two were the ones who had dragged him clear of the room he had entered through, and there was one standing near the door, wearing a suit and tie, although there was a gun tucked inside his gray jacket.

Everything about the man screamed intelligence operative.

Then there was the woman. Her hair was still in a severe bun, but she had exchanged her pantsuit for a dark one, although Kris was having a hard time making out what color it was, exactly.

"Well, Kris, I really hoped it wouldn't come to this." She approached him, pulled out a flashlight, and shone it in his eyes one at a time. "But you had to play the hero. We didn't expect you to be on our trail as quickly as you were, which explains the Miami fiasco. I hope you don't think less of me for it."

"Hey, it was pretty good for an on the go operation," Kris answered, coughing and tasting blood in his mouth. "But then, you can't really put a plan in place for someone like me."

She drew a pistol—a 1911, her favorite—and pressed it to his knee, eliciting a sharp intake of breath from him.

"I'd say we're doing a pretty good job of it," she answered, a small smile playing on her bright red lips.

"Oh, yeah," Kris said, eyeing the rest of the group. "Four dead in a hotel across the street, plus a nice big hole in your window. I have to figure there are going to be a few questions about that."

The suit in the corner put on a pair of glasses before speaking. "None of the questions are going to come close to exposing our presence here."

"CIA, right?" Kris asked, spitting the blood out of his mouth before continuing. "Let me guess, your name is Lynch, and you were sent here to...contain the situation? Sure, the local cops aren't going to be able to penetrate your firewall, but you wouldn't be sent over to deal with a couple of nosy detectives, right? This position has been exposed, and after so much money was poured into making it a secure location in the middle of New York, the plug is going to be pulled and this cell is going to be dispersed. The moment your budget is reviewed, a lot of questions are going to be asked about why so much money was poured into a security company that's right across the street from where four unaffiliated mercs were gunned down. The Appropriations Committee might not be the brightest bunch, but they're not stupid."

Lynch stared him down and finally let himself scowl. "I don't like him."

"He grows on you," Claudia assured him, turning her attention back to Kris. "Well, he can. If he wants to. But then he goes off to be a crusader for mankind, and that makes you think he's gone off the deep end. You were made for this sort of life, Kris. You could be working with me, making a mint and making an actual difference in the world. But no, he wants to deliver presents to kids instead."

The CIA operative shook his head. "You don't think he actually—"

"Do you have any other way of explaining the kind of technology we have on our roof?" Claudia snapped, shaking her head.

That confirmed where the sleigh was. Kris settled into his chair and let his face go blank. The zip ties keeping his hands behind him were too tight for him to slip out of, at least as his hands were. He shifted his hand around. Not the most pleasant option, but one he had fallen back on in the past.

They would know he was trying to escape. Dislocating his thumb was loud enough that one of them was bound to hear it. He needed to time it with a little something more.

"Which provides me with a nice little segue into why you're here," Claudia continued, looking at him as she pulled a few errant strands of hair away from her face and tucked them back carefully. "That sleigh is a nice little piece of cutting-edge tech that would make all the consequences you just named worth it, which means that if you start talking and letting us know how to use it, there will be no need for you to do anything else. Hell, give us the blueprints and you can drive the one we have. You know, once we've verified them."

"That's all you need?" Kris asked, looking around the room. "Just someone to show you how the controls work? Is that it?"

"More or less," she answered. "The blueprints would actually be a lot better since we don't really want to have to take the beast apart to reverse-engineer it. Besides, we want there to be something for our engineers to test their prototypes against."

"That makes sense," Kris noted.

"So, where did you get the tech, Kris?" she asked, leaning closer. "It's years and years ahead of what we have ready to go in our labs and more than what the Chinese have going. I know you didn't get it from the Russians since they've been trying to use the North Pole and haven't been able to. I mean, you could have stolen the designs, but you couldn't have built it yourself."

"That also makes sense."

"So, you stole the thing already built and ready to go, which means someone's putting those babies together, and you stole one to do your little deliveries. Actually, that was pretty ingenious. So, where did you get it from?"

Kris nodded, then cleared his throat and took a deep breath like he was convincing himself that this was a good idea. Claudia and Lynch leaned forward like they were expecting him to start talking.

"It was made...by a bunch of magical elves," Kris finally

said. It wasn't technically a lie, although the Workshop had done most of the work.

Claudia smiled in that way he'd always thought was a sign of affection from her, but as it turned out, it only appeared when she was having fun. She had hoped he wouldn't break easily, and Kris didn't have time to brace himself before the butt of her weapon crashed into the side of his face with enough power to knock his chair over.

Kris groaned in pain as he forced his left thumb out of its socket, the clang of the chair hitting the floor covering the sound.

"Never start with the head," Lynch advised as the pair of goons pulled Kris back upright. "The victim gets fuzzy and unable to answer questions. That was the reason we stopped waterboarding people. Oxygen deprivation can lead them to tell you truly insane things, and they halluci-nate other things. It ends up making anything they tell you suspect."

"So, how do you guys at the CIA interrogate prisoners?" Claudia asked, inspecting his eyes to check for any sign of a concussion.

Of course, considering his manner of entry, he prob-ably already had one, but there was no time to get into that. He couldn't feel any of the usual signs of a concussion, which meant it couldn't be that bad.

"We usually use chemicals," Lynch replied. "We've gotten amazing results by developing an addiction and nursing it for all the information we could ever need. Doesn't matter, though. We don't have any of the necessary barbiturates to get him talking."

"What, you didn't come prepared?"

"I didn't expect to have to interrogate a prisoner. If you want, we can move him to one of our black sites in the city and do it properly, with doctors around to make sure our 'treatment' doesn't end up killing him. Since the controls on that fucking thing are biometrically locked to him, killing him might not be the best way for this to turn out."

The man had a point.

"His parents," Claudia noted. "Of all the people in the world, they're the only two he holds in any regard."

Kris tensed. She wanted a reaction from him, but he doubted she would be getting the one she was hoping for.

"Go on," Lynch answered.

"They live in the Bahamas. We could use them to get him to talk."

Kris laughed, shaking his head.

"Something I said funny?" Claudia asked.

"Only that we dated for years, and you still don't know me."

She tilted her head. "I mean, you did quit your career to go and deliver presents to kids, so I think that was already firmly established."

"You never did look into my files, did you? The times I was caught didn't stand out to you?"

Claudia narrowed her eyes and didn't reply.

"Go. Find my folks. Put them through about fifteen different kinds of hell. Kill them if you like. You know already all that's going to do is piss me off more, and you'll discover that anything you do to them will be turned on you a hundredfold. So, go ahead."

He was bluffing. He had been captured in the past, but it had never gotten to the point where his family was threatened. Or her, for that matter. They had been close enough that her capture would have mattered to him back in the day.

But it was enough. A hint of doubt flickered across her face as she turned to look at Lynch, which distracted the two mercs behind him. Both took a few steps forward. They had no plays and weren't sure what to do next.

Kris' mangled hand slipped out of the restraints, and he grunted as he pushed his thumb back into place. It hurt like a bitch, and he let the pain rush through his body.

"I'd tell you guys to kick jingle bell rocks, but why tell when I can show?" Kris asked, pushing up from his seat. He shoved the mercs toward Claudia and the CIA goon and jumped over to the table where they'd laid his gear out.

In a single swift motion, he drew the pin out of one of the smoke grenades and tossed it toward them.

"I always wanted to say that," Kris said with a soft chuckle.

CHAPTER NINE

Their reaction time was about what Kris expected it to be. Their weapons turned to him the moment smoke started filling the room, giving him just enough time to grab his submachine gun and hit the floor before the air above him exploded with bullets.

Milliseconds passed as he forced his battered body into a corner of the room that was filling up with smoke.

"Get down here, the rest of you!" he could hear Claudia shouting into a radio. "We've got a situation developing!"

If that wasn't the understatement of the century.

It at least gave him something to shoot at. Kris raised his weapon and opened fire. The bullpup had never been his favorite design, but it was proving helpful in his current prone position, shooting up at his targets. He heard one shout of pain from the cloud of smoke, but he couldn't tell if the hit would take that person out of the fight.

"Why are you going outside?" Kris shouted and stood, pulling the magazine out and slapping a new one in while collecting his pistol and the rest of his gear. "Haven't you heard? The weather outside is fucking frightful!"

He was angry. That was the only explanation for this sort of behavior. The rage was the only thing keeping him on his feet at this point, and he would fuel it incessantly as he drove himself toward the door, which the others were retreating from.

One of the goons hadn't managed to get out yet, or maybe he was covering for the ones who were retreating. Kris collided with him hard enough to drive him into the wall.

The drywall and framing collapsed under the weight of both men hitting it, sending them into the next office. Kris used his position and momentum to hammer his elbow down on the man's head, knocking it into the floor as he reached for the combat knife he could feel was belted over the man's body armor.

He pulled the weapon out and drove it straight through the Kevlar. Not the easiest of cuts, but he thrust the blade deep into the man's stomach with the full weight of his body.

"Stay down," Kris ordered. "Leave the knife in and wait for the medics and you'll live. Keep fighting and you'll die. You choose."

The man stared up at him, nodding quickly as Kris pushed to his feet, collecting the merc's pistol as he did, and moved toward the door.

The stairwell was clearly marked, and the doors had conveniently been left open, likely from when people had rushed down to see what was happening.

There was a fair bit of hall between him and it, though,

and he could see at least seven mercs rushing up to see what all the fuss was about.

There was no cover on the way to the door, not unless he stopped in an office between him and the stairwell.

He pulled out one of the flashbangs, tossed it down the corridor, and backed away just in time for it to go off. His ears were already ringing, and the bang only sounded like popping bubble wrap at this point. Kris was already heading out of the room, shouldering the P90 before tossing his last smoke grenade down the hall. It quickly filled with the pungent smoke.

"If you didn't want lead for Christmas, you shouldn't have pissed me the fuck off!" he roared, letting the rage rush through his body as he sprinted toward the newly arrived mercs, who were firing blindly down the passage.

Staying low and on the move was enough to keep him from getting hit. They dropped one by one, barely seeing him before being shot or stabbed into submission. The P90 clicked empty as he approached the last one, who was trying to retreat through the door of the stairwell. He gripped the man by his Kevlar vest, lifted him off the ground with a powerful roar, drove him through the door, and threw him over the edge. The man careened down three flights before crashing into the stair rails.

"Ain't no snowdrift to catch you there," Kris whispered, wincing at the impact. He was sparing those he could, but when he was in combat, it felt like something took him over. That something wanted no quarter and would give none.

When Kris shook his head, he felt a tweak in his neck, so he refrained from making that move again. There were no mercs waiting for him on the stairwell, which was a little surprising but not unexpected. Three other stairwells led to the roof, plus two elevators. They knew where he was going, and they would wait there for him to come to them.

Not that he really had much choice. Kris pulled the empty magazine out and tossed it, then slapped his last one into place.

After one flight of stairs, the adrenaline started to seep out of his system, reminding him of all the pains and aches he'd been trying to ignore. He could only take so much punishment. There was a first-aid kit in the sleigh if he could just get to it. Well, after that, he would have to spend most of the night heading across the world and doing his job.

But he needed to take this one step at a time.

He pushed the door open, and the New York winter wind gusted in like an icy embrace. He kept his weapon trained on the area around him, waiting and hoping for someone to break into his line of sight.

"There he is!"

Kris dropped to the roof and rolled to the side as bullets tore through the space he had occupied less than a second before. He shot in the direction of the hail of fire, but he knew he wasn't likely to hit anything he wasn't aiming at. It was enough to make them run for cover, though, and Kris pushed to his feet and scrabbled for a position that could give him a better view of the roof.

There were plenty of outcroppings that provided him with cover, but one in particular caught his eye—a camouflaged tarp that covered something that looked very familiar.

"Santa Claus is coming, baby," he whispered. The bullpup was mostly empty, leaving him only five rounds and a pair of pistols. Not the odds he had been hoping for, but then, this whole operation had been a litany of improvisation. He had to keep the act going.

Kris circled around, firing at the stairwell head that at least three of the mercs were using for cover.

None of the rounds hit anything, and Kris soon dropped the empty P90 and drew one of the pistols. It had no suppressor, which meant it was the one he had picked up from the merc he'd knifed. The rounds burst out of it quickly as he moved toward the sleigh.

Kris pulled his last flashbang, took the pin out, and lobbed it at the three men in the stairwell head. It wasn't the throw of the century, but it got the job done. All three scrambled out of their position, and Kris picked them off.

There would be more of them coming. The only reason there were no more now was that he had bulled his way through. So far, the tactic was working for him.

He gripped the tarp over the sleigh and dragged it off with all the power he could muster, revealing the familiar dark figure of the advanced stealth vehicle he only called a sleigh because of the tradition surrounding it. It looked like a bird of prey, or maybe a stealth ship out of a sci-fi film, perched and ready to fly as he moved to the door on the side. Sure enough, it looked like the biometrics had kept anyone from entering it, and the self-destruct had prevented the thieves from trying to force their way in.

A quick check to make sure nothing else was tying the

sleigh to the roof was all he could spare as he moved to the door and pressed his aching hand, still bearing the zip tie, to the ID panel.

"Confirmed," said the tiny screen. "Identity: Kris Kringle, St. Nicholas."

He smiled and stepped in as the door slid open for him.

"Stop right there, Kris!"

He froze in place, his whole body ticking in time with his heart rate. Claudia was right behind him, and he didn't need to hear the menacing click to know she had a weapon of some kind pointed at the back of his head.

"Turn around," she directed. "Slowly."

Kris did as he was told, inching his way around. She was on her own, with her 1911 in hand and pointed at him, a blank look on her face as she took a step forward.

"Drop the gun," she growled.

Once again, he did as he was told, letting the weapon drop and deliberately kicking it her way.

She took another step forward as something that looked like pain twisted her face.

"Damn it, Kris!" she shouted, keeping her weapon on him. "We fucking had it made! We were going to be rich together! Enough money to live like royalty and only taking easy work for the rest of our lives! Why the hell wasn't that good enough for you?"

Kris stood his ground, trying to wrap his mind around what she was saying.

"We loved each other," she said, shaking her head and pointing the weapon a little more vigorously at him. "We were happy, and you gave it all up to be fucking Santa Claus. How the hell does that happen? Show me the math.

How does one of the deadliest mercs in the world end up delivering presents to kids on Christmas?"

She was trying to find a reason not to kill him, and he couldn't think of a single good one.

Kris shrugged his shoulders, feeling a twinge of pain in one. "You weren't there on the ground. I was. I saw their faces, Claudia. It's like... Have you ever done something so horrible, so nightmare-inducing that you couldn't live with yourself anymore? That made you want to punch yourself every time you saw your face in the mirror?"

"Get a fucking therapist! That's how most of the rich and powerful in this country make it through all the horrifying shit they do!"

He shook his head. "Don't you think I tried? I put on a brave face every day for years. I had myself fooled until the nightmares started. Penance was the only way it could work without me putting a gun in my mouth. This is it; this is my second chance."

She stared at him for a few seconds, then took a deep, shaky breath.

"And this is *your* second chance," he said. "I'm not going to stop because you have a gun on me. You're going to have to shoot me, but I'd really appreciate it if you didn't."

She narrowed her eyes and barked a laugh, one even she was surprised by as she lowered her weapon.

"You know I was just bluffing, right?" she asked. "About your folks."

"I know," he answered. "So was I."

She laughed again, but it had a bitter sound to it as she looked toward the elevators and stairwells around them.

"Get the hell out of here, you idiot," she whispered, her voice cracking.

He wanted to ask her to join him and give her the whole second chance he had been offered, but as he took a step forward, the door slid shut again and the engines powered up, whining and shaking the aircraft as it took off.

CHAPTER TEN

The first aid kit in the sleigh did its job. A lot of people would spend the next couple of weeks in the hospital after experiencing what he had, but there was a job to do.

He was feeling a lot better, besides. There was no need for a trip to the hospital. Still, Kris found himself moving a lot more gingerly as he directed the sleigh through its paces, heading from city to city, making sure the presents were delivered on time and with as much stealth as possible.

Given that the Workshop was backing him, the possibilities were almost endless.

There was one present Kris wanted to deliver personally. It was a quick stop, but one he felt was necessary.

He had known what was needed beforehand, of course. The girl had been on the list, after all, and would be getting what she deeply desired for Christmas, but after her little brother had asked for something for her instead of himself, Kris felt as though his personal touch was required for the job.

He descended, limping a little since his right leg was still gimpy as he collected the present dispensed by the sleigh and left it in place under the tree.

It was a stand with a wig of thick brown curls, one of the best. He'd checked, knowing the price was well above what her parents would be able to afford. She was too old to believe in Santa Claus, of course, but that wasn't what mattered. He left it in place, with a smaller package next to it.

That one was from him, although the tag had the girl's name.

The kid had asked for something for someone else instead of himself. It seemed like the sort of behavior that needed to be rewarded whenever he saw it.

Kris looked around, making sure none of the alarms had been set off by his actions before pressing the button that would recall him to the sleigh.

It was far from his last stop for the night, and he had a long way to go. Of course, the tingling feeling in the pit of his stomach and the smile that wouldn't go away no matter how hard he tried would keep him awake and lively for the rest of the long flight.

"Clear in Miami?" asked a voice on the radio.

"All clear," Kris answered.

"Then you're good to go for the Caribbean. We're still clearing your flight path over Central America, though. All in all, we're on pace to break last year's record for speediest delivery."

"Like we did last year," Kris noted. "And the year before that."

"Whatever you're doing to that sleigh looks to be working. Have fun out there, St. Nick."

It was the only day of the year he let them call him that.

It had been a long night. He had followed nightfall across the planet, making it last until he found himself near the North Pole. The sleigh was a lot lighter now that the presents were all with the children, so it was a quick flight back to where the nights were still going to take a while.

A few months, from the look of things.

Still, there was something comforting about piloting the sleigh into its secure new stable. He wasn't going to let it be stolen again.

Not on his life.

Kris found himself smiling as he climbed out, making sure all the maintenance checks were running and would be fed to the computers in his office to ensure he knew of any repairs that needed to be done.

Not today, though. It was Christmas Day, and he was going to bask in the glory of a job well done. It had taken a little more work this time than the previous ones, but that was the nature of the job. For him, at least.

"You look like shit, Nick."

Kris turned to look at Valy, who had fallen into step with him.

"Yeah, well, it's been a long couple of days. I think I'm going to sleep until we need to open the Workshop for business again.

"Are you going to tell me why you look like you just lost a fight with a meat grinder?"

"I already told you—"

"Yeah, yeah, you had an accident while you were working on fixing the sleigh right before takeoff. We all heard the story. We don't believe it, but we figure you'll tell us when you're ready for us to know and no sooner."

Kris nodded as he picked up and donned the sling he had discarded on his way as he delivered the presents. He slipped his arm into it with a soft and unintentional sigh.

"Well, I hope you don't hold your breath while you wait to hear the real story," Kris told him as they headed into the common room, where the elves were working their way through bottles of champagne and Christmas treats in celebration of another year's job finished.

"So, you admit something *did* happen," Valy noted. "And you know we elves can hold our breath indefinitely, right? We don't need to breathe to survive."

Kris looked around the room as he claimed a ginger-bread cookie shaped like a Christmas tree.

"You're shitting me!" he finally exclaimed. "Tell me you're kidding."

The elves exchanged glances and broke out laughing.

"You're all getting coal next year. Just saying," Kris growled, shaking his head.

Valy grinned and offered him a glass of champagne. "That being said, we're all really happy to have you as our St. Nick. I can't imagine anyone doing the kind of job you were able to pull off."

"I feel the same way," Kris answered, raising his glass. "Here's to one hell of a year, and to having a much better one next year. You guys have all earned your vacation time."

Everyone cheered, then Valy opened another bottle and sprayed the contents all over the room.

"You know, after you've cleaned this mess up," he added, collecting another couple of cookies before leaving the room to let the elves get back to their celebration. He always got the feeling that they were never quite able to let loose when he was around. Like he was the boss, and they didn't want to show him how hard they could party.

They would join their families once the Workshop closed for the season, most of them heading down to Canada to visit the folks who had retired from their positions. A couple of clans had spread out in the deeper reaches of the Arctic that would be welcoming visitors for the season as well.

It was on Kris to keep an eye on the place until they returned, ready to get back into the job again.

Once the door in his office closed, he moved to his chair and sank into it with a low groan that was a mix of pain and pleasure. The seat was comfortable enough that he could sleep in it with no problem. He had spent several nights in it instead of on the sofa when he needed to sleep in the office due to one crisis or another instead of heading to his living area on the far side of the Workshop.

There was little else to do for the next couple of weeks until he needed to start gathering the lists again, and Kris found himself staring at the screens, which showed beaches, snowy mountains, and a half-dozen other vistas like they were just outside his window.

His penance was far from complete, but it was one more year added to the tally. A sense of emptiness he couldn't explain came along after every season was over.

His eyes fell on the desk in front of him when he realized there was a wrapped present on it, bearing his name. There was no indication as to who had left it for him, although he could guess that it was one of the elves before they went to the party.

It seemed like something they would do.

He attacked the wrapping like he was ten years old again and looking forward to getting his hands on a new baseball mitt. There was nothing like it inside. It was a thick mahogany case with gold chasing but no other markings.

Kris lifted the gold latch, tilting his head as he inspected the contents.

It was a silver 1911 Colt with pearl filigree and an ivory grip, designed to fit into his hand perfectly, Kris noted, picking it up. It was an exact replica of the pistol he'd given up when he pushed his life of death behind him.

There was a note under the pair of empty magazines inside and he pried it free, still gripping the weapon like he was afraid it would dissolve the moment he wasn't touching it.

And you say I never answer you.

Love,

W

There were many ways that could be read, Kris thought, raising an eyebrow as he inspected the 1911 and read the note again. He didn't recognize the handwriting. It wasn't from one of the elves. It couldn't be. Was he going crazy?

"Nah," he muttered as he put the weapon back into its velvet cradle and closed the case.

EPILOGUE

Christmas day. Odd how the feeling was so different this year than it had been in the past.

She was a few years past the general excitement that came with the day, but Amy wasn't going to let that dampen Billy's excitement.

There were some things people didn't need to be in a hurry to dismantle.

That being said, it was one thing to think about it, and quite another to be happy about Billy beating her door down at the crack of dawn to try to get her to wake up.

"It's Christmas!"

"No shit!" Amy shouted back, pushing up on her bed. "Say it louder so the whole neighborhood can hear you!"

"Language!" Dad shouted from his room. They weren't happy about being woken up by Billy's excitement, but there was apparently no help for it.

She groaned as she pushed out of bed, and a wave of dizziness hit her when she stood up. Amy was used to it, so she just gripped her desk until the feeling passed, then collected the medications she needed to take before breakfast and downed them quickly with a hefty gulp of water from the glass Mom had put next to her bed the night before.

She remembered to do it every day, which was kind of impressive.

Amy went to her door when Billy started beating on it again.

"You had better be announcing that the British are coming," Amy growled as she pulled the door open.

Billy was a predictable mess. He wasn't going to settle down to get his hair brushed for a while, which meant it would look like he was straight out of a jungle safari until at least lunchtime.

"Santa was here last night!" he shouted as loud as he could.

"Was he really?" Amy asked, rubbing her eyes. Billy grabbed her hand and started dragging her to the living room. "You catch him on the camera traps you left out?"

"No," he said, eyes falling but lifting again quickly. "But I believed he would come through! Come on!"

When she didn't move, he emphatically repeated, "Come *oooooonnnnn*!"

He wasn't going to be dissuaded. Their parents had left their room as well and were heading to the living room to look at the presents.

It was mostly the way she'd left it the night before after helping her folks wrap the presents, but there was something different.

Something new. She narrowed her eyes when she saw a

present that looked suspiciously like a human head next to a smaller package.

Billy whooped, jumped over the couch, and rushed to the presents.

"It's for...*yes!*" he shouted, carrying the suspicious package over to her. "This is for you! I asked Santa to bring it, and he did!"

"You asked Santa to bring me a present?" Amy asked, inspecting the gift and glancing at her parents, who looked as inscrutable as always.

"See, I told you!" Billy announced with a broad grin. "You have to believe!"

"Sure," Amy whispered as she pulled her little brother in for a hug and felt his hands run over her bare scalp before wrapping around her neck. "I believe."

The story continues with book 2, *Christmas Kringle: Coming to Town*, available now at Amazon and through Kindle Unlimited.

Grab your copy today!

AUTHOR NOTES

First, thank you for not only reading this horribly inappropriate Christmas story, but also reading my author notes in the back.

If you haven't read any of the stories that started in my feverish brain before this, suffice to say I can find certain things so funny, or irrationally fun, that I just have to work on the project.

Like this one.

You see, the cover for this story I picked up last year when I was traveling between Australia (you know, when we were allowed to travel) and Hong Kong. The artist is Jake Caleb and he was selling pre-mades off of his Facebook group. I found this interesting because Jake had already been doing dozens and dozens of covers for LMBPN Publishing and I hadn't realized he was doing this stuff off on the side.

(Look up JCalebDesign here: https://www. jcalebdesign.com.)

It was RIGHT AFTER Christmas 2019 when I saw this

cover and I loved it. I mean, who doesn't love a kick-ass Santa Claus? Seriously who? This guy has a sorta six-pack and tats. You can't get more macho than that.

(Yes, I know that just dated myself. I'll save you the trouble, I'm over fifty but still some ways to sixty.)

Anyway, I loved the image and bought it, figuring that we could turn that image into a story and the story that ended up happening is the one you just read.

So, cover first, story later was how this book was created. It happens more often than you might think. Creatives like myself can be inspired by just an image.

I named the book the way I did because if this story is well received (I'll know if I have been bad or good by how many reviews I get, and how many five stars...or one stars... I am given in my stocking at your favorite online bookstore.)

So, if enough of you enjoyed this story and want more and we (the team here at LMBPN) get the non-coal variety of response (or at least me... Let's throw the non-coal in my direction please), I think we will make a present with a new book in the series every Christmas going forward that we can.

And then, some of you will read it and share it with their family. Oh wait. You can't. Sentences such as 'Blo-ho-ho me' are in the text. Well, perhaps you share it with your teenagers. Ok, the older teenagers.

Man, when I die, I am going to get a tongue lashing for putting this book out. This is assuming I hit the pearly gates. If I happen to go the other direction, I'll probably get a high-five.

Let's face it, if you know anything about my books and

have read my pen-name Michael Todd (Protected by the Damned) this will be the story I am LEAST worried about. It's not like there is open sex in Michael Todd books, but there is plenty of very politically incorrect discussions.

I already have to work through the cursing discussions regarding The Kurtherian Gambit when I bite the big one. I'll have to stare solemnly at the angel explaining my mistakes and really try hard not to come back with 'But they were funny!'

Tough Crowd.

Anyway, I say all of that to say THANK YOU from myself and everyone here at LMBPN Publishing for Christmas 2020.

I refuse to allow COVID to take away the fun of the Christmas Season.

Ad Aeternitatem,

Michael Anderle

CONNECT WITH THE AUTHOR

Connect with Michael Anderle

Website: http://lmbpn.com

Email List: http://lmbpn.com/email/

https://www.facebook.com/LMBPNPublishing

https://twitter.com/MichaelAnderle

https://www.instagram.com/lmbpn_publishing/

https://www.bookbub.com/authors/michael-anderle